THE
MESSENGER

THE
MESSENGER

TIM SPITZACK

OAKTARA

WATERFORD, VIRGINIA

The Messenger

Published in the U.S. by:
OakTara Publishers
P.O. Box 8
Waterford, VA 20197

Visit OakTara at
www.oaktara.com

Cover design by Muses9 Design
Cover image © iStockphoto.com/main street, genekrebs
Cover image motorcycle © by Davvi, Flickr.com

ISBN: 978-1-60290-230-5

For
CAITY, ALY, JAKE, and JENNA

Four of the greatest blessings in my life

⌘⌘⌘

And to all of the people who fled a small town
in search of fame or fortune
but have since discovered the treasure they left behind.

Acknowledgments

First of all, I give thanks to God for His love and faithfulness (John 3:16, Romans 10:9). I also wish to thank the handful of people who read my manuscript and offered sound advice and strong encouragement—Lynn Ashby, Laura Evansen, Carla Johnson, Becky Ward, Tharren Keith, and my father, Maynard Spitzack—and to OakTara for helping make this book a reality. My deepest debt of appreciation goes to my bride and best friend, Jil. It is only through her constant support, encouragement, and excellent editorial critiques that this book is what it is.

⌘⌘⌘

Once in a lifetime
a story will change your heart
and your perspective....

1

The sun was just beginning to burn the dew off the lilac trees beneath John Jenkins' second-story apartment window when he stepped out of the door and onto the wooden landing of a freshly painted staircase that descended fifteen feet to the ground below. His hand instinctively grabbed the rail and supported his weight as he bounded down the flight of stairs in two- and three-step leaps.

At the bottom, parked beneath the staircase, was his new Harley-Davidson Sportster. He paused a moment to admire the shiny chrome that complemented the jet black polish of the bike he had received from his father and stepmother just six weeks earlier, when he'd graduated from the University of Minnesota. He loved the bike. He loved the power it had and the way it made him feel when he leaned hard into the corners of the open highway. But most of all, he loved the sense of freedom and independence ignited inside every time he turned the key, kick-started the machine, and heard the engine roar to life.

"You should walk to work. The exercise would do you good," bellowed a voice from behind the bushes, tugging Jenkins back from his vain thoughts.

The voice was that of his landlord, Bob Carlton. Carlton owned the Ace Hardware store in town and had been renting the second story of his refurbished Victorian home for the past three years to supplement his declining income. Jenkins rarely saw the man dressed in anything but a brilliant red Ace Hardware shirt with his name stitched over the left breast pocket, and tan Dickies, and today was no exception. If anything else covered Carlton's middle-aged, overweight torso, it was a plain white T-shirt. And he always wore white socks and black, hard-soled Red Wing work shoes, even with shorts.

Jenkins smiled wryly at Carlton as he jumped on his bike, kick-started it, and quickly twisted his wrist three times, revving the engine loudly with each turn. "Walking is exercise for old people," he shouted over the thunder of the engine. "Besides, I get my exercise running from the ladies." His booted foot shifted the bike into first gear as his hand quickly squeezed and released the clutch, thrusting him forward, spraying gravel in the direction of Carlton.

"In your dreams, college boy," Carlton called back, shaking his balding head, his bushy eyebrows forming a V in his contempt.

Jenkins could feel Carlton watching him as he exited the driveway and turned right onto Second Street, the main artery leading to the commercial corridor of Marquette, Minnesota.

Second Street was a wide, paved thoroughfare that ran directly parallel to the expansive Mississippi River. It tightly hugged the contour of the land, which consisted of a rollicking series of high bluffs and deep valleys. The view from atop the bluffs—of the panoramic splendor of the river valley—was breathtaking. Blanketing the slopes and stitched together by barbed wire was a patchwork of farmland, which freely and generously reflected the earthen hues of each season. On the eastern bank was Wisconsin, with its lush hardwoods and black-and-white dairy cows. Nestled in the recesses of the valleys were red and white farms with large, boxy barns, silos, corncribs and tool sheds. Feeder creeks and a winding series of rust-colored gravel roads ran between the farmsteads, oftentimes paralleling each other.

It wasn't long before the wind was tussling Jenkins' ebony hair over his dark-lens sunglasses. As he descended from atop the bluff, he began to casually notice his surroundings: the brilliant yellow day lilies planted heavily along a wrought iron fence, the canopy of mature oak and maple trees over the street, and the stark shadows produced by the bright morning sun that stretched out long across the road in a mosaic design. Then his eye caught sight of a home with a fence that needed a fresh coat of paint, another with high grass and overgrown bushes, and yet another with missing shingles and sagging soffit. His wandering mind whisked him back to his home in Eden Prairie, an affluent, finely manicured suburb of Minneapolis an hour and a half north of Marquette. His face creased with amusement as he shook his head back and forth and pondered the contrast of lifestyles.

In a matter of minutes Jenkins entered the downtown district of Marquette and was engulfed in two- and three-story brick edifices that had marked time and held history for nearly a century and a half. Upon his arrival in town, Jenkins had read as much history about the town as he could find.

Marquette had sprung to life when the Mississippi River served as the central source of transportation for goods to the upper Midwest. It had been settled by European immigrants, mostly German and Scandinavian, who were searching for a new and better life. When they landed on the shores near what is now Marquette, they found the soil of the river valley to be dark and rich and fertile. They quickly abandoned passage further north to till the land and plant wheat and corn and other cash crops.

As homesteads began to dot the horizon, an ambitious young merchant from Detroit named Nathaniel Olson built a simple wood-frame home on what was now Second Street and stocked it with dried goods, farming supplies, and other necessities of life. He lived on the top floor of the home and used the lower level as his mercantile and as a post office.

Not long after, the Hansen brothers, a large and broody set

of twins from Missouri, built an elevator to collect the farmers' bounty, weigh it, and facilitate its transport to other markets. The elevator was so successful that steamboat pilots made regular stops nearby to pick up and deliver cargo and passengers. The wide, easy bend in the river near Marquette proved to be an easy landing point for the pilots, and since they made scheduled stops there, it meant more people arrived weekly. The landing did more than anything else to ensure that the fledgling community grew into a bustling town.

Today the commercial strip was six blocks long, north to south, along the west bank of the river, which now served merely as a picturesque backdrop for the town. The Mississippi was still very much a working river and home to tow boats and barges that laboriously hauled goods on its wake, but the merchants and townspeople who lived within earshot were, for the most part, disconnected from it. The only time they saw direct profit from the river was when pleasure boaters from the Twin Cities of Minneapolis and St. Paul and others from the surrounding area tied off at the public dock and strolled into town, looking for an ice-cream cone, or a cold beer and a sandwich.

As Jenkins drove along, he studied the names of the stores that made up Second Street: The Pizza Corral, Don's Butcher Shop, The Marquette Pharmacy, The Corner Cupboard, The Marquette Cinema, Joe's Bar and Grill, and Donna's Beauty Salon. To him, these unimaginative names were indicative of the simplicity of the town.

Halfway down the street, at the corner of Second and Main, was the *Marquette Messenger*, a weekly newspaper, published every Wednesday, with a circulation of 2,161, nearly two-thirds of the households of the town. The newspaper office was one of the oldest buildings in town, evidenced by the cornerstone that bore its name and date of establishment, 1858.

Jenkins parked his bike in the diagonal stall closest to the front door, dropped the kickstand, and hopped off. In two steps he was up on the sidewalk, and another two brought him to the door, which he vigorously pulled open before sauntering inside.

"Hey, Rach, how's it goin'?" he asked in a flirtatious tone. He couldn't help but smile when he saw Rachel Collins each morning, because she was pretty and bubbly. Just one year his junior, Rachel had a large, vivacious smile, auburn hair, and brilliant blue eyes that flashed back at him every time he greeted her. She has been working at the *Messenger* as a receptionist and typist since her senior year at Marquette High. She was offered part-time work following a three-month school-to-work program administered by the high school and came on full-time the week following her commencement ceremony.

"Things are well," she said, then continued, "for me." The implication in her voice reminded him that he had been reprimanded the past week for his constant tardiness to work.

"Oh, I must not have heard the rooster," he said sarcastically, now scanning the room for his boss.

"Oh, brother," she said, rolling her saucer-like eyes high into her head.

Jenkins returned the exaggerated expression, grinned, and slowly swung open the wooden gate that separated the reception area from the newsroom, an area just large enough for three desks with computers, a production table, fax machine, and copier. He walked quietly to his desk, which was separated from the other two only by freestanding office dividers. At those desks were Margaret Miller, the production manager, and Frank Rhode, advertising manager. Both gave him a mischievous smile when they bade him good morning, which made him wonder what they knew...and he didn't, yet.

"Is that you, John?" queried a voice from an office on the other side of the newsroom. The voice was that of Steve Berg, editor and publisher of the *Messenger.*

"Yeah, ah, good morning, Steve," he yelled back.

"I'm glad you could join us this morning," said Berg, now standing in the doorway, his arms crossed high to his chest and his gaze firmly fixed on Jenkins.

Berg was a fair man and a good mentor for Jenkins because he drew out the best from him and his other employees. Berg has owned the newspaper for twelve years, honing his own journalistic skills and transforming a mediocre publication into one that won many accolades and awards. His writing and editing skills garnered respect from his colleagues, and his business acumen the respect of the townspeople.

"I'd like to see you," Berg said sternly, then disappeared into his office.

⌘⌘⌘

At the same time, the first telephone call of the day broke the morning silence. When it rang a second time, Berg glanced at his clock and saw that it was eight-twenty, the time Rachel normally went to the post office. Just as the tone of the third ring pierced the air, he quickly grabbed the receiver, perturbed that no one else had picked it up.

"*Marquette Messenger*, Steve Berg," he said in a low, commanding voice.

"Steve, good morning, this is Don Pittman. How are you?"

"Fine, Don, fine. How are you?" he replied, assuming that something newsworthy must have happened to motivate the sheriff to call him this early in the morning.

"I'm okay, thanks," Pittman said. "Say, I've got some information to share with you that I think you might be interested in hearing."

"Okay, what is it?" said Berg.

"Well, I just found out Mr. Gutzman died."

"Who?"

"Gutzman. Alfred Gutzman. You know, he lived on the first farmstead just north of the city limits."

"Oh, sure, of course. I'm sorry to hear that. How'd he die?"

"Heart attack, I guess."

"That's too bad." Berg waited to discover why Pittman was sharing this information with him. Normally the paper received all death notices from the director of one of the two funeral homes in town.

"Well, I thought you might want to write a story about him for your next issue. I'm sure you're aware that he did an awful lot for this community, and I think people should know about all he's done. Besides, his death also has an interesting twist."

"Is that right? What is it?"

"It's where we found him. In the Oakhaven Cemetery— between the graves of his wife and son."

"Really? That is interesting."

⌘⌘⌘

Jenkins was happy the phone call was for Berg. The conversation had given him time to get to his desk and prepare for the day, as well as come up with another excuse for being late. The first thing he did was check off another day on his calendar. *Three hundred and twenty-three more days,* he thought as he made a mark fully across the day's square with a thick, black felt-tipped marker. Counting the days to when he expected to resign from the *Messenger* had been a daily ritual for him. Although he enjoyed his job, he felt restless and uninspired at the small paper, which seemingly held no future for him. However, he was also a realist and knew he needed at least one year of newspaper writing experience to garnish his resume and provide him with the clips required to apply for a position at a daily newspaper. Jenkins had his sights set on the *Minneapolis Star Tribune*, the *St. Paul Pioneer Press*, and the *Chicago Sun-Times*.

He also knew he wasn't the only college graduate who had used this paper as a stepping stone. Rachel had filled him in on the trail of young reporters in the *Messenger's* history—and Berg's amazing attitude toward them. Rather than begrudging the fact he had to train someone new every few years, the publisher had chosen to take the high road in providing them the training they'd need to succeed in their next career opportunity. Jenkins knew he was lucky to work for and with a seasoned newspaperman like Berg.

"John, will you come here please?" said Berg shortly after ending his phone call.

"Sure." Jenkins quickly arose, walked across the room, and into Berg's office, which was small but well organized and brightly lit.

No words were said as he passed through the doorway but he could tell Berg was angry by the way the corners of his mouth drooped. Jenkins avoided direct eye contact with him as he pulled a chair to his desk.

"That was Sheriff Pittman," Berg said, getting straight to the business at hand, assigning Jenkins story leads for the upcoming issue. Most weeks Berg gave him two or three stories to write, in addition to the copy he was expected to turn in from his coverage of various meetings, including the county board, city council, and school board. "He told me about an elderly man, a farmer, who was found dead this morning in the Oakhaven Cemetery, slumped over the grave of his wife and child."

"Was he murdered?" asked Jenkins, both startled and excited. *At last I might get a real story.*

"Murdered?" replied Berg, appearing astonished at the

inquiry. "No-o-o," he said, dragging out the vowel. "We're in Marquette, remember? His name is Alfred Gutzman, and he owned the farmstead just north of town, past the city limits. He apparently died of a heart attack."

"Oh," said Jenkins, quickly losing interest in the prospect.

"I'd like you to write an obituary about him. He was a well-respected man in the community and supported many programs and activities in Marquette."

"An obituary!" Jenkins couldn't help but snap back. "That sounds like an interesting lead for a Friday."

"Welcome to community journalism," Berg quickly retorted, looking annoyed at Jenkins' tone. He exhaled a breath, then said more quietly, "It gets better. The other article I need by Monday is a piece on the Marquette Days parade, complete with photos."

"Pulitzer material," said Jenkins, resigning himself to the fact that two simple stories stood in his way of enjoying the upcoming weekend with his college buddies bar-hopping in the Twin Cities and taking in his first Twins game of the season. "I'll get right to work."

The bounce was less pronounced from Jenkins' saunter as he made his way back to his desk, pondering his assignments.

Okay, two stories. Two easy stories. A slam dunk. Let's see—the parade is at eleven. Starts at the intersection of Second and Vine. He leaned over, unbuckled the strap of his camera bag and opened it, hearing the familiar sound of Velcro separating from itself. He pulled out his digital camera, turned it on to make sure the battery was fully charged, and then checked a side pocket for the spare battery. *I'll show up at quarter 'til, snap the usual shots, and then I'm out of there.* He grabbed the canary yellow flyer announcing the parade route and event details, folded it in thirds, again in half, then slipped it into his camera bag.

Now, Gutzman. I can't believe I have to write an obit on an old dead farmer, he complained to himself. *Died in a cemetery. Wow! At least they didn't have to take him far to plant him.* A faint smile cornered his lips at the thought of his morose joke.

Gutzman. Alfred Gutzman. Jenkins reached for the phone book while booting his computer simultaneously. He thumbed through the white pages until he reached the Gs. *Garner, Gimms, Goodhue, Gunther, Gutzman. Ah, here it is. Alfred Gutzman. Rural Route Three, Marquette.*

Jenkins rolled his brown tweed-paneled chair to his computer, laid his hand on the mouse, and clicked open his address book. An hourglass dotted a sunny Caribbean beach scene as the program loaded. The address book appeared, still showing the last contact he made: Denise Fletcher, secretary at Marquette High School. He clicked back to the main screen and scrolled down until he came to the Ws. He scrolled a bit further, spotted the number he was after, picked up the phone, and punched the keys.

"Wabasha County Medical Examiner's office. May I help you?"

"Hello, this is John Jenkins from the *Messenger.* Is Doc Clark in?" he said in an informal tone.

"Yes, I'll put you through," said the receptionist, her voice never rising or falling.

"Doctor Clark. May I help you?"

"Hello, Doctor Clark, this is John Jenkins from the paper. Do you have a moment to talk?"

"Sure, John. What can I do for you?"

"I'm calling to verify the death of Mr. Alfred Gutzman. We just received a report from Sheriff Pitman that he died this morning of a heart attack."

"Actually, he probably died around seven-thirty last night, but nobody found his body until this morning, just after six."

"Can you tell me the cause of death?" said Jenkins as he grabbed a pen with the promotional inscription *Marquette*

10

Pharmacy—A Feel Good Place and scribbled down the time of death on a yellow legal pad that he always kept by his phone.

"Sure, I was called in early to examine the body. All signs point to cardiac arrest."

"Anything unusual about it?"

"No, nothing unusual. Except for the fact that his truck was found at his home. He must've walked the two and one-half miles to the cemetery. He was eighty-eight years old. His old heart simply gave out on him."

"Okay. Thanks, Doctor Clark. I appreciate your time. Have a nice weekend."

"Thanks, John. And you as well."

"Steve," Jenkins hollered from across the room in the direction of Berg's office, "did Pittman say where the funeral will be?"

He waited a moment for a response but none came, which wasn't unusual as Berg rarely held a conversation across the office floor. Jenkins walked the handful of steps to Berg's door and poked his head around the corner. "Excuse me, Steve. Did Pittman say where the funeral will be?"

"Yes, at the Breckman and Fallwell Funeral home. You can ask for Mike Fallwell. He should be able to give you the details."

"Great, thanks. Do you have his number?"

"Did you lose your phone book?"

"No."

"Check the business listings. It should be there."

"Gotcha," said Jenkins, quickly pulling his head back from the door before Berg could see his face sour at the remark. He returned to his desk and found the phone number.

"Breckman and Fallwell," answered a female voice on the other end of the line, in a low, lifeless tone.

"Hello, this is John Jenkins with the *Messenger.* I'm calling to verify information on the Alfred Gutzman funeral. Is Mike

Fallwell available?"

"Yes, one moment please."

"Hello, this is Mike," answered Fallwell in an unusually upbeat manner, his pitch so emphatic and loud compared to the receptionist's that it caught Jenkins by surprise.

"Mr. Fallwell, this is John Jenkins from the *Messenger*. I'm calling to verify service information on Alfred Gutzman. Do you have a minute to talk?"

"Sure, John, sure. How are you?"

"I'm fine."

"How's Berg? I missed him at Rotary last week. Give him a hard time for me, will ya? Tell him he's been elected to serve on the park clean-up committee."

"Really?"

"No, but it should get him to next Wednesday's meeting."

"Okay," said Jenkins, trying to sound amused. "I'll tell him."

"Great. Now about Alfred Gutzman," said Fallwell, not giving Jenkins the space to ask another question. "Alfred Gutzman was a kind soul. A fine man. There are few like him. He attended my church for as long as I can remember. St. Paul's Lutheran. 2520 Pine Street. And that's where the service will be. Monday. 10:00 a.m."

"Does he have any surviving relatives?" Jenkins chimed in at Fallwell's first pause.

"Actually, no. Alfred was an immigrant—from Hamburg, Germany, I believe. Came here in '45, just after the war. Married a Marquette girl, Mildred Knutson, and they had only one child, Frederick. Frederick died in Vietnam, in '67. We provided final arrangements. Mildred, God rest her soul, was killed when that awful tornado ripped through town in '85. You've probably heard about it. Took out a good section of the north end of town. Tragedy. Anyway, he never remarried, so no next of kin that I'm aware of."

Jenkins could hear that Fallwell got winded from his fast manner of speech. He pictured the funeral director as an overweight, nearsighted man in a blue pinstripe suit, resting on the back legs of his chair, feet stretched out.

"Anything special about the service?"

"No, I don't believe so. Pastor Terrell would be able to tell you more. Pastor Glen Terrell. Here, I have his number. 465-5623. That's 465-LOVE. Easy to remember. He's a great pastor and knew Alfred well. You should call him, too. I'm sure he'd be able to tell you more about his background."

"I might do that," said Jenkins, knowing he already had enough information to write the obituary and that he wasn't going to put forth any additional effort on the article. "Thanks. I appreciate your time."

"Sure, sure," said Fallwell. "And don't forget to tell Berg about his committee assignment."

"I won't forget. Thanks again."

Jenkins looked down at his legal pad. The page was about two-thirds filled with nearly illegible scratches: name, address, age, time and place of death, occupation, and family and service information. *That's about all I need,* he told himself as he hit the space bar of his keyboard to clear his screen saver and doubleclicked the icon for his word processing program. As a blank document appeared, he grabbed his maroon and gold University of Minnesota mug, adorned with the face of a cheeky gopher, got up, walked to the coffee pot, and poured a cup of java, noticing its light caramel color and faint aroma. He longed for a dark, rich cup of coffee from an outlet like Caribou or Starbucks, places he visited frequently in high school and college to socialize with friends and girlfriends.

He retraced his steps and sat down, setting his mug on the corner of the oak-veneered computer armoire. Perching his writing tablet on his easel, he began to construct the obituary.

Gutzman Found Dead in Oakhaven Cemetery

Alfred Gutzman was found dead Friday morning in the Oakhaven Cemetery, 1854 Pine Street. Wabasha County Sheriff Don Pittman discovered his body at approximately 6 a.m. near the grave of his wife and son. Wabasha County Medical Examiner Rick Clark said Gutzman died of a severe heart attack. He was 88.

According to Mike Fallwell, funeral director with Breckman and Fallwell Funeral Home, Gutzman emigrated from Hamburg, Germany, to Marquette in 1945, following WWII, and purchased a farmstead on the north end of town near the city limits. He married Mildred Knutson of Marquette and they had one child, Frederick, who was killed during the Vietnam War in 1967. Mildred died when the tornado of 1985 hit their homestead, destroying much of it, as well as a good portion of the northern end of Marquette. Gutzman has no living relatives.

Good enough, he said to himself as he saved his document and went on to his next article.

2

"Rachel, I've got a Chamber meeting at the country club. I should be back around one-fifteen," said Berg as he passed her desk while patting his shirt pocket for business cards and his trouser pockets for his car keys.

"Okay, have a good meeting," she replied with her usual pleasant smile.

Margaret, who worked a half day on Fridays, followed him out the door, and Frank was not far behind.

⌘⌘⌘

Just seconds after the door slammed, Jenkins appeared around the corner.

"Hey, Rach, I'm gettin' hungry. How 'bout you?" After only a few weeks on the job, Jenkins quickly learned that he could get by with taking an extra-long lunch break on Fridays when Berg was tied up with his Chamber meeting. Most of the time Rachel honored her one-hour lunch break by being back at her desk promptly within the hour. However, sometimes she indulged in a more leisurely lunch.

"Yeah, I guess I am. Corner Cupboard?" she asked.

"What are our options?" Jenkins replied, voicing his disgust for the lack of dining choices in town.

Marquette had few restaurants that offered a full lunch menu. Business meetings were typically held at the South Pines Country Club, which offered a daily buffet. The working class usually got a greasy burger at Joe's Bar or at the Marquette Bowling Alley, a thin-crust pizza or a plate of bland pasta with marinara sauce at The Pizza Corral, or went to the deli of the IGA grocery store for fried chicken or the special of the day, which was usually roast beef or turkey served open-faced with mashed potatoes on white bread. The Corner Cupboard was the only restaurant that offered some variety, and the only one that could seat over 50 at one time, other than the country club.

"I'll lock up," he said while Rachel grabbed the out-to-lunch sign, a white 8 1/2-by-11 inch piece of paper that was placed within a plastic sleeve, and taped it to the door.

The Corner Cupboard was just two blocks from the *Messenger* office, on the opposite side of Second Street, so the two walked, enjoying the warmth of the midday sunshine. As they approached the street, three cars sped by, which was unusual at one time in downtown Marquette, even at lunchtime. Then a dark blue Dodge Ram extended-cab pickup with large, knobby tires rumbled by, its frame high off the ground. In it was a weathered farmer in his mid-forties, dressed in a plaid shirt and wearing a Northrup King seed corn hat high upon his head, its bill pointing nearly straight up. As he approached the two, his right hand lifted slightly off the wheel to greet them. Jenkins didn't know the man, and he figured Rachel didn't either. However, in his short time in town he had already become accustomed to being waved at by farmers in big pickup trucks. He didn't acknowledge the man, but Rachel lifted her arm high in the air to return the gesture.

The rear tire of the truck was barely past them when Jenkins took his first step into the street. His second step landed just behind the truck, and he strolled casually across the street to the other side. Rachel waited until the truck was completely by them before following him, running slightly to catch up.

"Hey, what did Steve say this morning? Gonna lose a vacation day?"

16

"No, it's cool. Luckily he got a phone call to get his mind on other things."

The brief conversation carried them to within thirty feet of the restaurant. Standing outside the door, smoking a cigarette, was Marty Brandenberg, a State Farm Insurance agent who works three storefronts down. Brandenberg, dressed in a gray suit with a starched white shirt, was an avid supporter of youth athletics and of the *Messenger* because of its coverage of local sports. He was also a strong advertiser for the paper, often running a quarter page ad each week.

"Hi, Mr. Brandenberg," said Rachel. "Are you having lunch today?"

"Hi, Rachel. John." He nodded at both of them. "Yeah, Milly is waiting for me inside while I feed my habit before my stomach."

Brandenberg laughed at his own remark, and then his laughter turned into a rattled, wheezing cough, which he shielded with the back of his hand. He took one last long drag on his cigarette and let the smoke seep slowly out of his nose and mouth. Flicking the butt near the curb, he opened the door, letting Rachel and John enter before him.

John winced at the strong odor of the insurance agent's cigarette still on his breath and clothing.

Milly, Brandenberg's secretary, was seated near the front window with her nose buried in her menu.

A brown sign encased in a flimsy bracket on a thin metal pole instructed customers to seat themselves, so Jenkins and Rachel scanned the room for an open booth, finding one near the middle of the cafe. While they walked toward it, nearly everyone seated in the front section of the restaurant stopped what they were doing and stared at the pair before going back to their individual conversations. Jenkins could feel their eyes heavy upon him and resented the intrusion of his privacy. But the stares didn't seem to bother Rachel. She made eye contact with several of the people, offering a high nod and a large, toothy smile.

Fridays were typically the busiest day of the week at the Corner Cupboard. The owner, Kim Seifert, worked extra hard on Fridays to make her customers happy, hoping they might return on a Monday or Tuesday, her two slowest days of the week.

As the two sat down in their booth, each grabbed one of the ivory, plastic-coated menus tucked behind the napkin dispenser and condiments tray and studied them without saying a word. It was a futile gesture, because each already knew what they would order.

"Mom, guess what Miss Thompson told us today?" blurted out a kindergarten-aged boy who was having lunch with his mother in the booth closest to them.

"What's that, honey?" the mother replied.

It was clear from the mom's tone she was trying to sound interested, but was more tuned in to a more interesting conversation.

"She told Jimmy not to run with his pencil."

"Is that right?" the mom asked.

"Yeah, she told us that when she was a kid she saw a boy run with his pencil, fall down and get the pencil jammed right up his nose. He had to go to the doctors to get it pulled out," the boy said loudly, scrunching his nose and curling his top lip at the thought of it.

It was impossible not to overhear the exchange. Jenkins caught Rachel's eyes, and both of them grinned. Rachel quickly clutched her mouth with her hand to keep her laughter from spilling out.

"What'll it be?" asked the waitress, who suddenly appeared at the table, herself half smiling as she plopped down two plastic tumblers of water, one splashing over slightly. She was a pretty woman, in her late forties, with long blond hair pulled back in a loose ponytail. She was dressed in the same outfit as the other three servers in the restaurant, a brown and tan smock with white fringes around the arms and bottom hem. Her name, Sandy, was stitched over her left breast.

"Go ahead, Rach."

"Oh, okay. I'll have the 1/4 lb. burger with fries and coleslaw please," she said politely, while placing her menu back in its place. It was a meal she ordered nearly every time she ate there.

"Anything to drink?"

"A Pepsi, thanks."

"And you?"

"I'll have the Club and an iced tea."

"That's it?"

"That'll do it."

She scribbled the order on her pad, swung around, and ripped it off on her way to the kitchen's order-taking window. "Order in," she yelled to Hank, the cook.

"So what's the big news this week?" Rachel inquired.

"Oh, really earth-shattering stuff," said Jenkins, dryly. "Coverage of the usual meetings, and tomorrow I get to start my weekend by shooting pictures of the parade. You goin'?"

"Yeah, I guess. I've gone for as long as I remember. Why stop now? I'm meeting my sister and her kids. She always gets a good spot on Second Street near the starting point. Then we'll go to her house afterwards to grill hamburgers and watch a video."

At that moment Jenkins looked at the beautiful Rachel and pitied her for not having more exciting plans for the weekend. He forced a faint smile, trying to imagine what it must have been like for her to grow up in a place like Marquette, so void of any entertainment options. He regaled her with his plans for the weekend, then turned his head and scanned the restaurant.

But Rachel pressed for more information about the next

issue of the *Messenger*. "Writing about *anything* interesting this week?" she said as a bell rang in the background, followed by the deep, gravelly voice of the cook.

"Order up," he croaked to Sandy, who made her way across the restaurant, dodging elbows and outstretched legs jetting out between tables positioned too close together for a comfortable walking lane. With a wink to Hank, she grabbed the two plates of food, quickly pivoted, and arrived at their table as Jenkins was revealing the subject of his last assignment.

"Oh, not really," said Jenkins. "Berg's got me writing an obituary about some old farmer who died last night."

"Yeah? What's his name?" queried Rachel, who knew nearly every family in town, at least by name.

"His name was Gutzman. Alfred Gutzman."

The second his full name was uttered, both plates fell from Sandy's hands, one hitting the edge of the table and crashing to the ground, sending food flying in all directions.

"What did you say?" demanded Sandy, looking dazed and ghostly pale, her hands trembling at her side.

"What!" Jenkins shot back, giving her a quizzical yet perturbed look while wiping coleslaw from his pant leg.

"Who died?" she asked. "What did you say?"

"Ah, Gutzman. Alfred Gutzman," he stammered, now puzzled at her interest.

Sandy froze, turning two shades whiter. Her shoulders sagged, her mouth gaped open, and her eyes became fixed on a distant point no one else could see. She took a step back and her legs buckled; she fell onto the back of a chair behind her. She would have fallen to the floor had the chair not been there, grounded by a farmer in tattered, dirty overalls. She untied her apron and wildly flashed her eyes around the room until she made eye contact with her boss.

"Kimmy, I've got to go. I'm sorry," she said as she threw her apron to the ground and went running for the door, tears now streaming down her cheeks.

The commotion drew the attention of nearly all the other patrons in the restaurant, who watched her leave, then quickly looked back at the mess on the table and floor.

Jenkins and Rachel stared at each other in bewilderment. Jenkins couldn't make sense of the situation.

Then Rachel's eyes turned sad. "Oh no," she moaned.

"What was that all about?" Jenkins finally murmured, attempting to blot the stain on his pants with his napkin.

"She knew him. They were close. Really close. You better go and see if she's okay."

"What? I don't even know her!"

"John!" she said sharply. "You should tell her what you know."

"Are you serious?"

She didn't answer, but her glare said everything.

"Ah, okay," he replied, knowing she wouldn't drop the subject until he at least walked outside in a futile attempt to find the waitress.

Kim and another server appeared at the table, throwing apologies and stacks of napkins and damp rags at them as Jenkins stood up, squeezed past them, and headed for the door. As he stepped outside, he could see Sandy hurrying unsteadily down the street, stopping every few steps to wipe away the tears with her sleeve. Since he and she were the only two in sight, he walked briskly, occasionally running a few steps, to catch her.

"Hey, hey! Are you okay?" he called while still several yards away.

Sandy turned around, her eyes puffy and red, her cheeks streaked with black mascara tear lines. She eyed Jenkins for a minute, as if wondering what he was up to, then turned to continue walking, though now at a much slower pace.

"Sorry," said Jenkins. "I was just wondering if I could help."

With that, she took a few steps in from the street, leaned against the warm brown brick wall of the Marquette Pharmacy, and stared at Jenkins. Again, she wiped her cheeks with her sleeve and ran her thin fingers through her bangs, patting them against the side of her head as though attempting to compose herself and improve her appearance.

"He was such a good man. A wonderful man," she said, eyes again glistening with tears. "I can't believe he's gone. I just can't believe it."

"You knew him?" said Jenkins, fumbling for some appropriate words but finding none.

"Yes. Yes, I did."

"Would you like to talk about it?" asked Jenkins. Though the situation was uncomfortable, he was relatively confident his journalistic skills would help carry him through the awkward conversation. From his time in journalism school and his few weeks on the job, Jenkins had already become adept at asking questions and drawing out responses. During his interviews, questions rolled naturally off his lips, even the tough ones that many young journalists choose to avoid. In J-school, he was taught to write down his questions before entering an interview. However, it was a practice he rarely applied. He quickly discovered he worked better without a prepared list, thus making his interviews more natural, more personal.

Sandy nodded in response to his question and continued walking, giving him permission to follow her. He was surprised she was willing to talk to him about what was troubling her and searched his mind for what to say. Then he remembered the advice of one of his favorite professors, Bruce MacIntosh, a man who played the professor role to the hilt by wearing tweed jackets and penny loafers, and who always smelled of pipe tobacco. He would often preach to his class about the importance of talking to those who had just experienced a tragedy. Dramatically pointing his finger just above the students' heads, he would say, "Don't be afraid to talk to the widow. You need the information, and it helps them with their grieving process."

The two moved along slowly together, not saying a word. There was a small city park near the river, just two blocks away, and they headed toward it. The park was nearly empty, except for a man at a picnic table who had just pulled a sandwich from a brown paper bag, and an elderly woman who was walking her little brown Dachshund on a short leash. They found a bench near the bank of the river and sat down, both staring at the water for several minutes before Sandy began to speak.

"I haven't always been just a waitress, you know." She glanced briefly at Jenkins, then focused her attention on the waves lapping the shoreline.

"Is that right?" he replied, not looking at her but rather allowing her some space.

"I was an English teacher when I first moved to town. At the high school," she said. "I was fresh out of college and so excited to get that job. It was great, you know. I was working. I was making money. I had my own apartment. It seemed like everything was falling in place for me."

Jenkins looked her way and nodded but still remained silent. He noticed she looked younger than he had remembered her from the times he saw her at the café.

"And then I met Andy. At first, he seemed like a dream come true. He was handsome, funny, and bright. Do you believe in love at first sight?" she asked.

"Ah, I'm not sure. Guess I've never given it much thought." Jenkins had never been in love. Although he had several girlfriends throughout high school and college, he always ended his relationships when the girl of the moment got too close, too personal. He enjoyed his freedom and didn't like having outside demands thrust upon him. He had broken up with his last girlfriend just three weeks before college graduation because she broached the subject of marriage. They had been dating for seven months—not long enough, in his mind, to begin such talk.

"Well, I never did, until I met Andy," Sandy continued. She had finally stopped crying and was beginning to talk more rapidly. "He was the math teacher at the high school and an assistant football coach. I remember the first time I saw him. It was my first fall in Marquette, at the varsity scrimmage. I was helping the Spanish club sell watermelon to raise money for a trip to Mexico. We were set up near the entrance of the football field, and all of the players came running by."

She motioned with both of her arms to punctuate the story. "One boy pushed another, and two of them came crashing down on our stand, and Andy was right there. He grabbed the boys by their jerseys and threw them toward the field. Then he looked me straight in the eye and flashed this great big smile. 'Sorry. Boys will be boys. I am sorry, but I gotta go.' I gave him a dirty look and began helping the kids pick up the mess, but I knew at that point that I was in love."

"Sounds nice," said Jenkins, who was beginning to wonder where this conversation was headed. He glanced at his watch while Sandy was looking away and noticed that it was a quarter 'til one. Fearing he was going to hear Sandy's entire life story, he decided to advance the conversation on his terms to find out if she was truly in need or if she was simply an emotional basket-case looking for someone who would listen to her story.

"I'm sorry, but what does your relationship with Andy have to do with Mr. Gutzman?" he asked.

The mention of Gutzman's name caused her eyes to well up again. "He helped me when I was in trouble," she said, her voice cracking.

"What kind of trouble?"

"Ask anyone in town. I'm sure they'd be more than happy to give you the full story." There was the sting of bitterness in her tone.

24

"I'm sorry. I'm not sure what you mean."

"I know. I'm sorry, too. You see, things didn't work out between Andy and me. Our relationship advanced in a hurry and, well, the next thing I knew I was pregnant." She folded her hands across her stomach, one over the other. "When I told Andy about it, he blew up and called *me* irresponsible and stupid. I guess, in a way, he was right. He abandoned me, and it hurt. I was twenty-two years old, pregnant, and very scared. I didn't know what to do, so I tried to keep it a secret, but it wasn't long before that was impossible, too.

"At the end of the school year, Andy left without saying good-bye. He didn't even tell me he quit his job and was leaving Marquette. I've never seen or talked to him since. I heard he's selling insurance up in Duluth."

"Wow, that's too bad. I'm sorry you had to go through that," said Jenkins, still trying to make the connection between her and Gutzman.

"Of course it didn't take long for my secret to become public knowledge," she continued, making quote marks in the air with her fingers for the word *secret*. "The long and short of it is this: the schoolboard met, the superintendent called me into his office, and I was out of a job. Not a fit role model, he said.

"As you can imagine, I was devastated. And my family was little help. Word shot through my hometown like wildfire. They weren't prepared to deal with it. So I went to my pastor. Pastor Terrell. Do you know him?"

"No. Well, I know *of* him," said Jenkins, surprised to hear his name for the second time that day.

"I went to his office one day in tears. He was meeting with Al Gutzman. He's an elder..." She caught herself. *"Was* an elder. I told Pastor Terrell I needed to talk but would come back later, but he insisted I sit down. He introduced me to Al, then asked him to excuse us so we could talk. I was so upset, though,

25

that I broke down in front of both of them and told my story.

"They were so kind. They just listened and held my hand. And when I was finished, they prayed for me. Right there, they prayed for me."

"They sound like neat men," said Jenkins, trying to sound sympathetic. The story was mildly touching, but not remarkable—or newsworthy. "So you stayed close to him because he was your church elder?"

"Oh, he was so much more than that. If it weren't for Al, I don't know where I'd be today. He took me under his wing and showed me more kindness and sympathy than I've ever been shown."

"How do you mean?"

"A few days after our talk I got a call in the evening. It was Al. He called to see how I was doing. I was a little embarrassed, so I told him I was fine. We made small talk and then I let him go. But he called me again about a week later. He said he had been thinking about my situation and that he wanted to help."

"So what did he do?"

"What *didn't* he do? He helped me pull my life back together. He helped me get a job when few people in town would even speak to me. He supported me financially for many years until I got on my feet. But more so, he helped me with my son, Josh. When Josh was young, Al would watch him so I could go to work or go shopping. As he grew, they'd go fishing, to a ballgame, all kinds of things. He has always been there for him; for us. He was like his grandpa."

Sandy sighed. "He was there when my parents weren't. Eventually, as Josh got older, they tried to reconcile with me, because they wanted a relationship with him. But they missed so much along the way.... Al saw it all."

Again Sandy fixed her gaze on the river. "How am I gonna tell Josh?"

Just then the town clock on the nearby courthouse chimed

one. Jenkins and Sandy looked at each other, startled.

"I'm sorry. I've carried on too much. We better go. You'll be late for work," said Sandy as they arose from the bench and walked briskly through the green grass and past a rusting metal playground set on their way back to Second Street.

"That's okay," Jenkins replied. "I'm truly sorry for your loss. It sounds like Al Gutzman was a nice man. I'm sure you'll miss him."

"More than you'll ever know."

The two walked along without talking until it came time for them to part.

"It's John, right?" she said. She looked a bit uncomfortable, as if just realizing she'd barred her soul to a stranger.

"Yeah. John. John Jenkins."

"I'm Sandy."

"I know," he said, pointing to the embroidered name on her smock.

She smiled. "Well, thanks for the ear, John Jenkins. I'll try to get your food on your table next time instead of in your lap."

Jenkins laughed as he looked down at his stained pants and then stretched out his arms at his hips, palms out, to proudly show the stain to the world.

Her expression grew serious then. "I hope this is all off the record."

"Of course," he said, somewhat surprised at the remark. "Of course it is. I'm glad we had a chance to talk. Hang in there." With that, he extended his hand, and she grabbed it softly. They shook hands, exchanged a small smile, and then went their separate ways.

3

Jenkins' alarm clock had been buzzing for over a minute before it roused him far enough from his slumber to roll over and slap it silent. Without opening his eyes, he burrowed deeper into the warmth of his covers, wishing he had shut his bedroom window the night before and longing for the extra blanket in his closet that he had taken off his bed only last week. The temperature had reached eighty degrees the day before, making it stuffy in his room when he went to bed, so he had opened the window wide to cool down his room and enjoy the evening breeze. Now it was frigid in his room, but nonetheless he drifted back into a deep sleep and his dreams captured him again….

"John, have you completed your essay?"

Jenkins was resting his head on a desk. He looked up and in the direction of the voice and saw that it was Sandy. She was wearing her waitress smock but was standing at the front of a classroom, like a teacher, holding out her hand toward him as if to receive his assignment. He looked around and noticed that about twenty high schoolers surrounded him; some looked like football players, some cheerleaders, and others just average faces.

"John, have you completed your essay?" she said again, still holding out her hand.

He looked down at his desk and on it was a sheet of paper containing only his name and one paragraph of handwritten text. He glanced around the room, noticing that the other students had written at least two pages each. He felt embarrassed and confused because he wasn't sure of the topic he was supposed to write on.

Just as Sandy was to ask for his assignment a third time, an elderly man walked into the classroom. He walked over to Sandy, smiled, and then looked at John and smiled at him as well.

"It's okay. It will come to you," he said.

Then he disappeared....

Jenkins' alarm clock burst forth again in a series of high-pitched beeps, spaced apart in one-second intervals. This time he heard it sooner and was quicker to disarm it. Blurry-eyed, he tried to focus on the clock. It read 8:22. He sat up quickly, thinking it was a workday and that he had again overslept. When he finally cleared the cobwebs from his mind and came to his senses, he realized it was Saturday morning. He flipped the switch to the radio position, plopped back down on his pillow, and slowly came to life as the beat of a hip-hop song broke the morning silence.

Another fifteen minutes had passed before Jenkins finally rolled out of bed. He stumbled to the bathroom, took a long, steamy shower, thought about shaving, and got dressed. He walked to his kitchen, poured himself a bowl of frosted cornflakes and grabbed the milk from the refrigerator. He unscrewed the cap, gave its contents a whiff, then doused his cereal, spilling milk over onto the countertop.

Jenkins' family had money. His father was a successful mortgage banker in Minneapolis and his stepmother an interior design consultant. However, you'd never know he was from a privileged family by looking at his apartment. His kitchen set consisted of a well-used Formica-topped table and two chairs.

His living room housed an old green couch, a faded leather recliner, a coffee table, and an artificial palm tree, all of which came with the apartment. On the wall opposite a large picture window was his sanctuary—a large-screen home theater system and stereo unit that likely cost more than all of the other furnishings together. His time in his apartment, which wasn't much, was usually spent in front of the TV, watching whatever sport was in season.

After finishing his cereal, he put the bowl in the sink, grabbed his camera bag, and headed out the door for the parade. It didn't start until 11:00 a.m., but he wanted to get there early and take the obligatory crowd and food vendor shots before it all began so he could hurry out of town immediately afterward.

Jenkins arrived downtown at a quarter after ten. The normally sleepy district was abuzz with activity. Food vendors busily set up their stands, while parade entrants made final preparations, lining up in the order they'd appear on the route. Parade watchers laid claim to the prime viewing spots on Second Street by setting up lawn chairs and placing coolers next to them. Everyone smiled and waved as they stood clustered in little groups, discussing their weekend plans.

Jenkins marveled at the degree of excitement the parade and surrounding activities created. Marquette Days, always held the first weekend in June, was the city's annual community celebration. The weekend was packed with activity. For the past dozen years the event had begun on Friday night with a softball tournament at the city fields—advancing teams played through Sunday afternoon. In addition to the parade, Saturday events included a pancake breakfast sponsored and served by the Rotary Club, a 5K fun run sponsored by All Star Sporting Goods, a pig roast at the VFW, and a sidewalk sale. Many families and church groups gathered together at the three largest city parks for a picnic, and the youth capped off the evening with a street dance. Colorful red, white, and blue light post banners promoting the event had been up for ten days. Most of the downtown merchants flew American flags outside their shops as well.

Although the street was blocked off, Jenkins wheeled his motorcycle around a barricade and made his way to the *Messenger* office. All street-front parking was off-limits, so he tooled behind the building and parked in one of two spots reserved for newspaper staff. During the week, Berg always used one of the spots. Jenkins knew that he and his family would be coming to the parade, so he took the other stall normally used by Frank, the advertising manager, who was typically the first staff member in the office each day. Jenkins also knew that Frank would be at the parade and would undoubtedly expect to find his parking spot free, but he didn't care. The spot was available to anyone on the staff who arrived early enough to get it.

Jenkins got off his bike, slung his camera bag over his right shoulder and headed for Second and Vine, the starting point of the parade, three blocks away.

"Hey, John, ready for a great parade? It looks like terrific weather," said Jake Herman, the town's mayor, as he shuffled busily by in his navy blue suit. He was heading for the parade starting point where his '66 red Mustang convertible was waiting for him. For the past fourteen years that he had been mayor, he had used his sportscar to chauffer the Marquette Days Queen and her two princesses. Today, seated atop the back seat would be Caity Bartelt, Alyssa Olson, and Jenna Richards. His car was the third unit in the lineup, following the Marquette High School marching band and the color guard.

"Sure am," Jenkins replied. He could see the mayor was in a hurry and wasn't offended at only receiving a passing remark.

Herman had always been very cooperative with Jenkins, especially during the bimonthly city council meetings. The mayor must have liked Jenkins, because he'd come to Jenkins' aid during his first council meeting after he'd asked a rather poignant question of a long-time councilman. The councilman demanded to know who was speaking, and when Jenkins identified himself, the councilman rolled his eyes. "Oh, that explains it. Another rookie." Herman had quickly defused the confrontation and made the councilman answer his question.

As Jenkins continued on down the street, he began to scout out photo opportunities.

"Hot dogs, no line. Get your hot dogs here," screamed a vendor who was already set up and open for business. "You look like you need one," he said, pointing a ketchup bottle toward Jenkins.

"No, but you'd look good in the paper. Give me a smile." He raised his Nikon to his eye, cupped its body with his left hand while adjusting the focus, and snapped off a quick shot.

"*The Messenger?*"

"Yeah," said Jenkins as he stepped toward the white cart with a red canopy and message board that read: *Hot Dog w/Coke—$3.*

"How long you been sellin'?"

"This is my sixth year at Marquette Days, but I've been in business for seven, since the summer I bought this beauty," he said, thumping the side of his stand solidly three times. "A new heatin' element, a new canopy, a new paint job, and I was in business."

"Expecting a good day?"

"Looks like a winner. Sun is shinin', people are out and they're lookin' hungry." He then turned his attention to an approaching family. "Hot dogs, no line. Hot dogs and a Coke. Three dollars!"

"Good luck," said Jenkins as he turned and walked away, knowing this picture would never make the paper.

In as little as fifteen minutes the amount of people crowding the streets had nearly doubled. Older children crisscrossed the street, chasing after one another, while mothers and fathers tried to keep a tight rein on their youngsters, which was difficult to do since their arms were laden with diaper bags, small coolers, blankets, and lawn chairs.

Jenkins was now having difficulty moving in a straight line and had to zigzag his way through the crowd. In front of him was a young family. The parents appeared to be in their late-twenties, and both were very attractive. The man was around six feet tall, had broad shoulders and a full head of thick black hair. His wife was tall, too, just a few inches shorter than he, and very slender. Her long, flowing blond hair seemed to reflect the rays of the sun. Their two-year-old daughter was perched high upon her father's shoulders. Her tow-white hair was curled at the bangs to keep it off of her face, and the rest was pulled back into a ponytail. She was dressed in denim overalls, blue and white tennis shoes, and was clutching a tiny American flag in her right hand.

Jenkins focused his camera on the family and waited until the mother looked up at her child before he fired the shot. He moved slightly out into the street, zoomed in on the child, and snapped another shot. Then he approached the family, identified himself, and asked for their names. As they were speaking, he glanced at his watch and saw that he had just five minutes before the start of the parade. Saying good-bye, he stashed his camera and notebook in his bag and quickly walked the remaining block to the starting point of the parade route.

For as many years as Marquette Days had featured a parade, it had been led by the color guard of the VFW, and this year the tradition continued. Milling around, smoking cigarettes and looking rather jaded, were four old veterans whose uniforms revealed signs of wear. Jenkins knew he wanted a shot of the vets marching with the flag, so he moved in closer while trying to frame the picture in his mind. He looked for the spot he believed they would begin their march and scanned for other objects that might help identify the scene to *Messenger* readers: a street sign, a building, or something of that nature.

"It's a shame Gutzman is missing this one. He always loved this celebration. It won't be the same without him," said one of the men, dressed in his WWII Class A Army uniform, his voice deep and raspy.

Jenkins snapped his head toward the conversation and approached them. "Did you say Gutzman?"

"Yes. Who wants to know?" demanded the vet.

"Oh, sorry. My name is John Jenkins. I'm with the *Messenger*. I'm sorry, but I couldn't help but overhear you. Were you talking about Alfred Gutzman?"

"Yes. Why do you ask?"

"Well, I'm writing an obituary about him for next week's paper, but I didn't realize he was a veteran."

"Well, actually he's—"

"There are probably a lot of things you don't know about him," interrupted another man, also dressed in a WWII uniform. Although he was undoubtedly in his early eighties, he looked very fit and rather distinguished in his pressed uniform, dress hat, and shiny black shoes.

"Like what?" Jenkins asked, disgusted with himself for not discovering this tiny bit of information about Gutzman.

At that moment, a Vietnam-era Army vet with three stripes up and three down on his shoulder barked an order and the men moved quickly into position.

"Meet me at Vets Park after the parade if you want to find out who he really was," said the aged soldier.

"Ah, sure. Okay, I'll meet you there," he replied as the color guard hoisted the flag and put the parade in motion.

Jenkins let his camera bag drop to the ground, flipped open the top, grabbed his camera, and ran out ahead of the procession. He missed the shot he had wanted and scurried to get into a position where he could fit all of the vets into the frame. Then he ran back to where he left his bag, retrieved it, and began shooting the other floats and action surrounding the parade: people laughing and pointing at parade units, kids getting their noses or cheeks lightly tweaked by clowns, street vendors selling their wares, etc.

It was the goal of the Marquette Days committee to have a parade that lasted one full hour—not a minute longer, not a moment less. Although Jenkins became bored with the event about halfway through it, he felt obligated to stay until the end. The last shot he took was of a clown dressed in gaudy, multi-colored clothing, mismatched stripes and large polka dots. Knit stockings were pulled up to his hairy knees, and he wore oversized floppy shoes and an orange baseball hat with an extra large brim. He had a large, red rubber nose on his brightly painted face, a *Messenger* newspaper carrier's sack draped across his shoulders, and an open umbrella that he was holding high in the sky.

Jenkins focused on the clown as he approached a pile of horse manure, left behind from the final parade entrant, the 4-H club. With perfect timing, Jenkins fired off a flurry of shots as the clown bowed to the dung, saluted it, collapsed his umbrella, which had a scoop on top, picked up the droppings, and hurriedly put them in his sack. The crowd cheered. The clown bowed to them, then shuffled on his way.

As Jenkins was making his way back to his motorcycle, his cell phone rang. He pulled it from his pocket, looked at the incoming number, and flipped it open.

"Hey man, what's up?" answered Jenkins.

"Dude, you still in Mayberry? You're not gonna make first pitch," said his friend who was calling from his apartment in downtown Minneapolis.

For three weeks Jenkins and three of his college buddies had been planning their weekend get-together. The afternoon was to start with tailgating in a parking lot near Target Field and then a beer on the plaza while listening to a band. After the game they'd drive a few miles to a pub in Dinkytown, the college village of the University of Minnesota, where they would hoist many glasses of beer, flirt with the college girls, and reminisce about their time together at the university.

"Relax, it's only noon now. I'll be there by two for sure." Jenkins glanced at his watch while doing the math to calculate his arrival for the 3:05 game.

"I know, man, but the steaks are thawin', and the beer's on ice. Don't be late."

"I'll be there."

Jenkins was excited for the weekend. He had been home only one time since he'd moved to Marquette and was eager to see his friends and his first Twins game of the year. He was also looking forward to seeing Marquette in his rearview mirror and re-immersing himself in the hustle and bustle of city life.

⌘⌘⌘

A short while later Jenkins was approaching the city limit sign, a spot on the highway where the speed limit jumped from 35 to 55 mph, when he remembered his promise to the old soldier.

Ah, he'll never miss me. He probably won't even show, he said to himself as he sped along, kicking his bike into a higher gear, trying to forget the conversation and turn his thoughts toward his weekend activities. As he cruised along at 70 mph with the sun warming his neck, he tried to recall the Twins' match-ups against the Brewers and thought about the pre-game party that he would enjoy with his friends. However, the solitary nature of cycle riding made it difficult for him to get his thoughts off of Gutzman. If he was in a car, he would have turned on the radio or put in a CD to distract him, but on his bike, he was left alone with his thoughts. As he sped down the road his conversations with Fallwell, Sandy, and the WWII vet swirled around in his mind.

It's a stupid obit about a dead farmer, he complained to himself. *I can't believe I'm even considering this.*

He peeled back the cuff of his leather riding jacket and looked at his watch. *12:17 p.m.*

I'll give him half an hour. Hear what he has to stay. I'll still have time for tailgating.

Glancing in all directions, he slowed down his bike and made a U-turn in the middle of the highway.

⌘⌘⌘

When Jenkins arrived at Vets Park, the soldier was there, sitting outstretched on an iron bench, tie loosened and hat in hand. Veterans Park was actually more of a memorial site than a park. A small swatch of land, some 60 feet wide by 120 deep, sandwiched between the Marquette Pharmacy and the post office. The land had once been the site of a Ben Franklin variety store, before it burned down on Veterans Day, 1978. When the city fathers learned the company had no plans to rebuild the store, they deemed it appropriate to erect a memorial to the town's military heroes on the site, once they acquired the land. The park now featured four marble slabs with the names of every man and woman from Marquette who paid the supreme sacrifice for the country. The names were alphabetized under each war, beginning with WWI and ending with the Iraqi War. On each side of the memorial, set at opposite angles, were two park benches. Leading away from it was a brick walking path. The area on both sides of the path was filled with flowers—mostly red, white, and blue chrysanthemums and daisies, now in full bloom—and a few small ornamental trees and shrubs. As

Jenkins approached, the vet turned his head slightly in his direction.

"I thought you'd forgotten about me," he said in a melancholy voice as Jenkins moved in closer and stood directly in front of him.

"No, I remembered," he said, holding out his hand. "I'm John Jenkins."

"Jerry Peterson."

The vet stood up and firmly shook Jenkins' hand, then both sat down, facing the monument.

After a brief silence, both men began to speak at the same time.

"I'm sorry, go ahead," said Jenkins.

"Al was a good man. I take it you never had the pleasure of meeting him."

"No, I'm afraid not. I've only been in town for about six weeks. How did you know him?"

"I've known Al for over fifty years," he said, rubbing his chin. "It's hard to believe it's been that long. You're young, so it's difficult for you to understand, but it's tough getting old and watching everyone you know and love pass away."

Jenkins could see that time had indeed attacked the vet's body. Jerry's face was creased with wrinkles, especially around his eyes, and his thinning hair was snowy white and wispy. His hands were peppered with age spots, and when he spoke he often cupped them together and massaged the backs of them, as if to rub away his arthritis. He was tall and trim, yet Jenkins knew he had trouble with his knees by the way he stood up and sat down, always keeping a hand on something solid to support his weight.

"Were you in the service together?" asked Jenkins, trying to speed up the conversation.

"You could say that. We were in the war at the same time. WWII. But we were on different sides of the line."

"How do you mean?"

"Exactly as it sounds, young man. You see, there's a history to old Al that few ever knew. He was a Kraut. Served in the German army."

"You're kidding?"

"No, I'm serious. He was the enemy...that is, until I got to know him. I'll never forget the first time we met. It was '46, just about a year after a handful of Marquette boys and I got home from Europe. This town lost over a dozen good men over there. Boys, really. Their names are there," he said, motioning to the WWII memorial slab. "They're also in my yearbook."

"We were having a few beers after a softball game at Harry's," he continued. "Well, it was Harry's then. Now it's Joe's Sports Bar. Anyway, we were dressed in our ball uniforms. We were hot and sweaty and drinking hard to celebrate our victory. We did everything hard in those days—worked hard, played hard.

"Then in walks this guy no one has ever seen before. Good-lookin' guy. Tall, brown hair, broad shoulders, around our age. So naturally we're staring him down, you see, trying to figure out who he is. We watch him as he walks up to the bar and orders a draft. Well, we were at a table near the bar and could immediately hear his German accent. He was trying to talk low and disguise it, but when you've gone eyeball to eyeball with so many of 'em in battle, you pick it up really quick. We all looked at each other, then Jonesy turns to him and says..."

Peterson paused and laughed to himself. It was as if a dark shade was being lifted from the recesses of his mind, peeling back years of aging and long-forgotten memories, and a new light began to sparkle in his eyes. "It was so many years ago. Or was it only yesterday?"

4

"You're a Kraut, ain't ya?" screamed a man over the din of a Sinatra tune crooning from a jukebox in the corner of the bar. The music was loud, as was the crowd, so few overheard his remark. But Gutzman heard it and chose to ignore it. He pulled out his wallet, opened it, gave some cash to the bartender, then grabbed his beer and headed for a small table near the pool table and cigarette machine.

Wooden chair legs raucously scraped the floor as four men pushed away from their table in pursuit of him.

As they caught up, the loudmouthed one said, "Maybe you didn't hear me! I said, you're a Kraut, ain't ya?"

Gutzman put his beer on a wooden ledge on the wall and stood tall, his shoulders and chest filling his shirt. "I'm from Germany, if that's what you're asking. But I'm an American now."

"American?" the loudmouth snapped back, stepping closer and standing so close that Gutzman could smell the beer and cigarettes on his breath. "You don't sound like an American. Does he, Jerry?"

"Not to me, Jonesy," Jerry replied.

"Nope," said one of the other men.

"Sounds like a Kraut to me," said the fourth man.

"Listen, I don't want trouble. I'll just leave," said Gutzman, his accent becoming increasingly pronounced under stress.

"That's a great idea," said Jones. "Why don't you go all the way back to der Führer land with the rest of them fascists?"

Although the war was over, its harsh memories were still fresh and alive in the hearts and minds of these young men who had experienced the horrors of battle. Fighting far from home on foreign soil, each had seen friends' lives cut short in bloody terror, and each carried deep scars...some physical, some emotional. They let the Kraut get out the door, then rushed outside after him.

"Hey, ever been in battle? Were you in the war?" shouted Jones, the shortest man in the group.

Jones had been a star shortstop for the Marquette Mavericks before the war. He was very competitive and very temperamental. His dream to play ball in college and then the pros had ended during a fierce battle overseas when shrapnel ripped apart his throwing arm.

Gutzman stopped. He looked in the direction of his car and knew they would reach him before he could reach it. Next, he scanned the parking lot, hoping to find someone who might come to his aid but saw no one. He turned and faced them.

"I don't want trouble. I'm going home." On the outside, Gutzman appeared brave and confident, but on the inside he was trembling, his heart pumping wildly with adrenaline.

"You got that right," sneered Jones as he balled up his fist and sent it crashing squarely onto the side of Gutzman's jaw.

The blow spun Gutzman around and split open his lower lip. With blood trickling down his chin he made a dash for his car, but Jones was right behind him and smashed his forearm into the back of his head, sending Gutzman to the ground in a cloud of dust. He writhed in pain and tried to get up but could only get to his hands and knees. Jones cocked his leg and gave a thundering kick to his midsection, which again sent Gutzman careening to the ground. Jones stepped forward to where Gutzman was lying and kicked him in the middle of his stomach, then spat on his head.

"Now you can go home, Kraut," he said as he turned and walked back toward the bar with his buddies, who were laughing and slapping him on his back.

"Another victory for the U. S. of A.," said Peterson.

Gutzman thought hard about running after him and quickly imagined what he would do to him once he caught him, but given the odds, he decided against it. He picked himself up off the ground, wiped the blood from his lip, dusted off his shirt and pants, and limped to his car.

⌘⌘⌘

Jerry Peterson was a farm kid, born and raised on a small dairy farm five miles west of Marquette. It was a farm that had been in his family for three generations before him, so the agrarian lifestyle was so deeply ingrained that he never considered anything but returning to it after he got home from his tour of duty.

At age twenty-two, he was still living at home with his parents, Vern and Irene. He often thought about moving out but always decided against it when he considered the inconveniences he would suffer. Prior to the first milking of the day, which began at 5 a.m., his mother would cook a hot breakfast, usually ham and eggs, for his dad, his two brothers, and him before they ventured out into the dawn to begin their chores. He knew if he moved out, he'd have to cook for himself, do his own laundry, and keep his own house, not to mention getting up earlier each morning to make it to the farmstead for the early milking, the first of three throughout the day. For now, he was content to live under his parents' roof until he found the right girl to marry. Someone who would tend to those duties for him.

The morning was cool and dark, and the dew hung heavy on the ground as the men silently made their way to the barn. Approaching it, they could hear the cows stirring and groaning, as if they knew it was time to produce. The sweet smell of hay and the pungent aroma of manure filled the air. Once inside, Vern flipped a switch that illuminated a handful of bare bulbs dangling from the rafters. He took his position by the nearest cow and began to extract the milk from the soft, pink udders. The brothers fell in line, oldest to youngest, and did the same. Not a word was said as the men milked the first few head of cattle.

"I was talking to Pastor Johnson after services yesterday," Vern finally murmured in the direction of Jerry. "He said he met a young man at the hospital the other night while making his visits. Turns out he got himself in a bit of trouble and got banged up." He paused as he moved to the next cow. "He's around your age. He's new to town and could use a friend. Pastor hoped that you might get to know him. Show him around. Introduce him to some of your friends."

"I guess I could do that," replied Jerry in a tone barely above a whisper, knowing his father had already volunteered him for the duty. "What's his name?"

"Alfred. Alfred Gutzman."

⌘⌘⌘

The muffled chime of Jenkins' cell phone broke the conversation. Jerry Peterson looked at him, smiled, and waited for him to answer it.

"Sorry," he said as he pulled it from his pocket, looked at the number on the display and then at his watch, which now read 1:20. He answered the call.

"Hey man, I can't talk right now. I'm with someone."

"With someone! You're supposed to be here. You're gonna miss first pitch," said his friend from Minneapolis. "Where are you?"

"I'm still in Marquette. I got tied up. Look, I'll just meet you at the park. You've got my ticket, right?"

"Yeah, I've got it. Dude, it's Saturday. You should be partyin', not workin'."

"I know. What section are we in?"

"Hang on," the voice on the other end said. "Ah, 119. Section 119."

"Okay, if I leave soon, I can still make it. I'll meet you there. Gotta go."

"Goin' to the Cities this weekend?" asked Peterson as soon as Jenkins slipped the phone in his pocket.

"Yeah, some friends and I are going to the Twins game today and tomorrow."

"Sounds fun. The Brewers, right?"

"Yeah, the Brewers," said Jenkins, again looking at his watch. "Listen, I've got to get goin' pretty soon. Did Mr. Gutzman fight in the war?" he asked impatiently.

"He did. He was a grunt just like me. Soakin' and freezin' in those stinkin' foxholes, trying not to get our heads blown off. Turns out we might have even fired some bullets at each other in a battle near Cantigny, France. Our boys fought hard in that one. Stopped 'em good. Saved the Brits that time."

"So how'd he get to Marquette?"

"By chance, actually. He was thumbing a ride from Chicago to St. Paul to stay with his uncle, who was living there and promised to help him find a job. He actually defected from Germany before the war was over. Said he loved the country but hated its politics. He told me the story over a few beers one night. I think it was the only time he ever spoke of it. He got

44

separated from his company and spent a few nights in a concentration camp. He said when he saw what they were doing there it made him sick to his stomach. He couldn't do what they ordered him to do, so he walked away."

"So the two of you became friends? How'd that happen? It sounds like you and your friends held some pretty deep animosity toward the Germans. Did you end up meeting him after your friend gave him the Marquette welcome?"

Peterson laughed.

"Not exactly. I recognized the name as soon as my dad said it. I was successful at avoiding him for a while, but our paths finally crossed, and that's when my attitude toward him changed...."

⌘⌘⌘

The Zumbro River was a wide stream that meandered its way through the wooded bluffs and farmland near Marquette before emptying into the Mississippi River. When winter finally surrendered itself to spring, the melting snow caused its current to become strong and swift for several weeks, usually in mid-April to early May. It was a time when the river offered its highest adventure and some of its best fishing.

Peterson and his friend, Earl Olson, loaded his cedar and canvas canoe in the back of his faded black '39 pickup and headed for the river access near the Leon Swanson farm, a few miles down a gravel road from Peterson's farm. It was a warm afternoon, and though it had rained the night before, a plume of dust kicked up behind them as they sped down the road, gravel spraying from the rear tires as they caught and gave way in loose patches.

Peterson hit the brakes hard and fishtailed to a near stop at a narrow dirt road that led about one-quarter of a mile to the river. He turned the truck toward the Zumbro and proceeded slowly, the two of them bouncing back and forth on the black vinyl seat as he maneuvered over a plethora of water-filled holes that pocked the road. The turnaround at the river's edge was muddy. Peterson worried for a moment that he might bury the truck in the mud but plunged ahead anyway. He pushed the gear lever to first and pulled the keys from the ignition.

He and Olson smiled at each other and jumped out into the mud. They untied the canoe, pulled it off the back of the truck, letting it drop heavily to the ground, then dragged it to the river. Olson ran back to the truck, grabbed two paddles and a wicker basket filled with salami and cheese sandwiches and beer, and threw them in the canoe. The two of them pushed the vessel from the shore, getting their trousers wet nearly to their knees, jumped in, and were caught up in the rapid current.

Springtime in Minnesota was unlike any other time of the year. Only those who have patiently suffered through the snow and bitter cold, and the short, dark days that winter in this region produces, could truly appreciate the beauty of it, and the effect it had on one's soul. It was a time when leaves miraculously popped from hard gray branches and the landscape exploded with a vibrant shade of green. Wildflowers burst with color—yellow, blue, lavender, white and orange— emitting their sweet fragrance. And the sun, which seemed to have scorned the living only weeks earlier, now climbed high in the sky to deliver its bright warmth.

It was a picture-perfect day, and the two friends were happy to be away from their chores and on the river. Since they weren't accustomed to speaking openly about beauty and matters of the heart, they were silent for the first several minutes of their paddle as they basked in the warmth and serenity of the day.

It wasn't long before the roar of the river drowned out the songs of the finches and the chickadees and aroused their imagination. They were headed for a stretch of rapids that looked long and hard and angry. The swollen river swirled and churned around boulders that were forever trapped in its grip. Last fall, Peterson had canoed this same stretch of river but had to get out and walk his canoe over the sharp exposed rocks because the dry summer had sucked the life out of the Zumbro. Now the full weight of the river was upon them.

The two gripped their paddles tightly and began throwing deep powerful strokes at the river. Olson was in front, frantically alternating his paddling from side to side. Peterson was perched in the stern of the canoe, bracing himself in with his knees and stretching himself to see around Olson while both paddling and holding his paddle firmly in the current as a rudder to navigate around exposed rocks and snags.

After several seconds of wrestling the raging water, they came upon a particularly fierce section clogged with downed tree limbs and boulders. Seeing no way around the conglomeration of wood and granite, Peterson steered directly through the middle, praying they would skim right over the tree branches.

The instant the canoe hit the branches, it skidded up on them. Olson pushed off to keep them from flipping over into the water. The canoe went over the tree limbs, but then crashed into a boulder, spun sideways, and capsized. Olson was able to grab hold of the canoe and float through the treachery, but Peterson was thrown into the tree limbs. His shirt became tangled in the brush, and the current began to suck him under. He thrashed his arms wildly, coughing and spitting out the water rushing into his throat, while trying to call out for help....

On the south bank of the river a fisherman had been casting into the current. He watched with amazement as the two shot through the rapids, thinking to himself that they were foolish to be in the middle of such nasty water. When he saw the canoe capsize, he dropped his rod and rushed along the brush-choked bank, partially disrobing as he ran, twigs and branches scratching and puncturing his skin as he made his way toward the accident.

Just as the man in the water was losing strength, the fisherman dove into the river up current and was able to swim out and free him. The two spun around in the current as they were pulled along through the tangle. When they reached calmer water, the fisherman flipped the nearly drowned man over, threw his arm across his chest, and stroked for the shore. Once there, the man's friend, who had beached the canoe and made his way back upstream, came running over and helped pull his friend from the river. The two laid him on his back and watched as he choked and gagged and spit out water.

After regaining his composure, the man the fisherman had saved rolled to his side and then pulled himself to his knees and cocked his head to see his rescuer.

"It's you?" he said as he made eye contact.

⌘⌘⌘

"So Gutzman saved your life?" asked Jenkins, surprised, as he marveled at the thought of it.

Peterson's eyes twinkled as he nodded in affirmation.

"As you can imagine, my attitude toward him changed dramatically after that day. I found myself a little more willing to accept him as a man, not an enemy."

"So the two of you became friends," said Jenkins, now intrigued with the story and wanting to learn more. Just then, his cell phone chimed. He pulled it from his pocket and looked at the screen, displaying a familiar number. He turned it off without answering it, but it reminded him that if he didn't leave soon, he would be late for the game.

"Your friend in the Cities?" asked Peterson.

"Yeah, sorry but I've really got to get goin'," he said while standing and extending his hand.

"Mr. Peterson, I really appreciate your time in telling me more about Mr. Gutzman. I wish we had more time to talk."

Peterson arose slowly, his legs shaky, and grabbed Jenkins' hand and shook it firmly. His mouth curled in a slight grin that conveyed the fact he wasn't finished talking about his old friend but that he understood that a young man has better things to do than sit and listen to an old man reminisce.

Jenkins put on his sunglasses, mounted his bike, and started the machine. He gave Peterson a nod as he drove north on Second Street, leaving him there with his memories and the rest of the afternoon to think about his cherished friend.

49

5

Jenkins' foot pushed hard on his motorcycle's rear brake pedal while his hand tightly squeezed the hand lever for the front brake as his reflexes worked in unison to avoid a collision with an approaching blue and silver Pontiac Grand Am. His body instinctively leaned away from the ensuing vehicle, which was now in a short brake skid with its rear tires squealing.

The driver maneuvered away from Jenkins by steering hard to his right, which sent the right front tire of the car bouncing up onto the boulevard. His face burned with anger as he shot a piercing glance toward Jenkins, who was now stopped on the opposite side of the intersection. He flung his car door open wide and stormed out. Dressed in a dark blue cotton work uniform, the man looked as if he had just finished a shift greasing machinery. His shaggy black hair bounced as he ran across the street to where Jenkins was standing.

"What's wrong with you?" he screamed, inching closer to him. "You completely blew through that stop sign."

Jenkins' heart was racing. He could feel it pulsating in his neck and making a thunderous sound in his ears. "Ah, sorry. My fault," were the only words he could mutter, knowing he was at fault indeed.

Noting that Jenkins was visibly shaken by the incident, the man's anger quickly subsided. "Hey, are you okay? You're not hurt, are ya?"

"No. No, I'm fine. Listen, I'm really sorry. I guess my mind was on other things."

The man looked at him and then across the intersection at his car. "Don't worry about it," he said, while walking across the street to examine his vehicle. "I don't think there's any damage."

Jenkins followed closely behind him and watched as he inspected all four tires first, then the front quarter-panel over the tire resting on the boulevard. Next, he dropped to his hands and knees and looked underneath the car. Seeing no damage, he got up, wiped his hands on his trousers, dusted the dirt from his knees, and repeated himself. "I don't think there's any damage." He climbed into the car, started the engine, and revved the motor, the rusting muffler telling its age. He shifted to reverse and slowly backed off the curb. "Watch out for yourself, now. That could've been ugly," he said through his window as he drove away.

Jenkins stood by the curb, trying to gain his composure. Images of his near accident flashed through his mind as he watched the car move slowly down the street until it was out of sight. He walked across the street, got on his bike, and drove down the block to the next stop sign.

On the corner was a large brick church, St. Paul's Lutheran. In front of it was a stout man in his late forties putting black letters on a white marquee, its glass door fully opened against the building. He wasn't yet halfway through his project when Jenkins read the fragmented message: *Funeral Service. Alfred Gu.* He quickly recalled his conversation with John Fallwell, the funeral director, about how Gutzman's funeral service was to be held at St. Paul's.

Jenkins sat at the stop sign and stared long enough for the man to feel his presence and make eye contact. He gave Jenkins a long look and then smiled and went back to his work. Jenkins sat there a moment longer until a minivan appeared behind him. He quickly turned left and parked opposite the church, got off his cycle, and walked across the street.

"Hello, I'm John Jenkins, with the *Messenger,*" he said, not really knowing why he had come across the street to talk to this man or what he would say next.

"Hello, I'm Pastor Glen Terrell," the man replied, followed by a short moment of silence during which the two men stood and considered each other. "I had to doublecheck my lettering because I thought I had spelled something incorrectly by the way you were looking at me a minute ago."

"Oh, sorry. I couldn't help but notice your announcement. You see, I'm writing an obituary on Alfred Gutzman for our next issue."

"An obit? I see. Did you know him?"

"No. I'm afraid I didn't."

"That's a shame. He was a wonderful man," he said, wiping away a bead of sweat clinging to his right brow. "I knew Al for many years and would be happy to share some information with you about him, if you'd like. I'm just about done here."

"I'd like that," Jenkins said, pushing his promise to his friends to the back of his mind.

"Great. We'll go to my study. It's cooler in there." He finished his lettering, which included the service date and time, and packed some letters scattered about back into their proper alphabetical slot in a small, brown cardboard box.

As the two approached the pastor's study, the phone rang.

"Excuse me, John. I have to get that. It's my secretary's day off. Please, have a seat."

"Thanks," Jenkins said, but opted to stand and browse the room.

The pastor's study was surprisingly large and housed an oak desk and matching library table, a mid-sized conference table, two filing cabinets, and a built-in bookshelf that spanned the entire west wall. Jenkins scanned the books, which ranged in subjects from the life of Martin Luther to fighting spiritual battles, and from marriage to death and dying. The walls were papered with a manly brown and beige sculptured print and were filled with diplomas, crosses, plaques with religious sayings, and photographs. There was one picture that caught his attention. It was of a young man in his twenties with dark, shoulder-length hair, sideburns, and a bushy moustache. He was posing with three dark-skinned men in front of a crude tin building that had a cross on it, and large, waxy palm tree leaves draping over it.

"That was my first parish," said the pastor as he approached Jenkins after finishing his call.

"Where was it?"

"Down in Columbia in a small fishing village near Cartagena. That's me in the middle. Back when I had more hair. Nice 'stache, huh?" Jenkins laughed. "It was in 1981. I had just graduated from the seminary and decided to give missionary work a try. I served in that village for three and a half years, and it was one of the most rewarding experiences of my life. I was able to help build that church and share the Gospel with people who've never heard its life-changing message. Are you a Christian?"

"Yeah, sure. I guess. I mean, I believe in God," Jenkins stammered, uncomfortable with the blunt question. He'd never given much thought to religion. His parents had taken him to Sunday school when he was a child but stopped when he was in the sixth grade, following their divorce. The only times he remembered going to church as a youth were on Christmas Eve, when he attended with his mother and grandmother. Now, as an adult, he found no time—or reason—to attend.

"Great, because that's really all God wants from any of us: to believe and trust in Him and His Son, Jesus, and for us to know that He loves us."

Jenkins just nodded, straight-faced. He could do without the religion talk.

"But we're here to talk about Alfred, right?"

"Yes." Jenkins clicked back into reporter mode. "I understand he attended church here and was an elder. Is that correct?"

"In fact it is. It looks like you've done your homework."

"Well, I ran into Sandy at the Corner Cupboard, and she told me a little about him."

"Yes, she would know. They had a very special relationship."

"How did you first meet him?"

"Unfortunately, it was under less-than-ideal circumstances," he said as he motioned for Jenkins to take a seat in front of his desk as he sat down himself. "I was new to town and was still getting my feet wet with this parish. I wasn't in town for more than three weeks when a terrible tornado hit our town. It was awful. It killed three people from our congregation, including Alfred's wife, Mildred. I'll never forget that day and meeting him at his farmstead as he was grieving her death...."

⌘⌘⌘

The sky was still a threatening muddy brown and spitting small amounts of rain when Pastor Glen Terrell approached the Gutzman farmstead. His window was rolled halfway down and he could feel the humidity quickly returning to the cool air of the summer storm. He looked to his right and could see the wide swath of damage the fierce tornado had created as it blazed through a cornfield. Then, peering to his left, he saw where it continued on through another cornfield.

In the middle was the Gutzman homestead, structurally intact but severely damaged. The house had a large hole in the roof and was missing sideboards and shingles. Most of the windows were blown out and pieces of glass lay scattered about, reflecting the rays of sun beginning to break through the dark clouds. Nearby the remains of a barn lay in a pile of large, jagged splinters, looking as if its center was removed, causing its sides to fall in on each other. Debris and both living and dead livestock were scattered across the lawn. Lying beside the barn rubble was a calf with a shovel handle driven straight through it. Except for an old black Labrador that was barking at soaked shirts and overalls waving to and fro on a laundry line, the scene was eerily quiet.

The windshield wipers slapped away at the intermittent drops of rain as Terrell wove his faded red Chevy Citation between the carnage and stopped near a pile of rubble where the garage once had been. Seated on the step of the back door entrance to the house was a man in his late sixties, slouched over with his elbows on his knees and his head in his hands, his thick silvery hair falling forward. Although Terrell had only met Gutzman a few times, he knew it was him.

As Terrell turned off the engine, he saw Gutzman glance his way, and then return to his same posture. There was a sinking feeling in the pit of Terrell's stomach as he got out of his car. At the seminary, he had been counseled on how to deal with death and the bereaved, yet he never felt adequately prepared when faced with real-life situations. Approaching Gutzman, Terrell dreaded every step. He prayed for guidance and searched his thoughts for what to say.

"Alfred," he said softly as he approached him.

Gutzman looked up with deep, sorrowful eyes and began to rise.

"Please, stay seated," Terrell said as he sat down beside him, with Gutzman shifting his position slightly to the right to make room. Terrell put his hand on the grieving man's shoulder, and the two sat in silence for several minutes— Gutzman in his sorrow, Terrell in prayer.

Then he finally spoke. "Al, I'm sorry for your loss."

"Thank you, Pastor," he replied, his voice cracking.

"I wish I had the chance to know her better. I understand she was a kind woman."

"Yes. She was."

It had only been a few hours since the ambulance had taken away his wife's body. Alfred was still in shock from seeing her lying on the floor in their living room, blanketed with glass and plaster.

He had been in the barn when he heard the downpour of rain stop abruptly, and then what sounded like a freight train coming toward him. He rushed out in time to see the tornado jump from the field to the top of the house, to the garage, and then over to the barn, which exploded behind him as he ran toward the house.

The force of the blast knocked him to the ground. The moment he reached the house and walked through the door, which was now hanging on one hinge, he knew something awful had happened. He paused before entering the living room, where his lifeless wife lay....

"It's all too difficult to understand," Gutzman said. "But I guess the Lord giveth, and the Lord taketh away."

Terrell was surprised to hear the man quote Scripture. In light of the circumstances, he wondered if Gutzman was speaking these words in comfort, or in mockery.

"Yes. It's impossible for us to understand why these things happen," Terrell offered. "We simply need to know that God is there for us, to help us through it." As the words rolled off his lips, he felt a twinge of uneasiness. Were these the most comforting words he had to offer? What did he know about death? He had never lost a loved one, especially not a spouse of nearly forty years. He desperately tried to think of more words of reassurance, but none seemed adequate, so he simply put his hand on Gutzman's shoulder again and squeezed it firmly a few times.

"Let's take a walk. I suppose we're going to have to discuss the arrangements," Gutzman said in reference to her funeral.

"Sure we can, but first I'd really like to hear more about her, if you don't mind."

The two arose.

Gutzman studied his property and shook his head in disbelief. A slight breeze blew in and jostled the damaged screen door behind them. He turned toward the sound of it, expecting to see his wife standing there, urging him to invite the pastor inside for coffee and pie. He was silent for a moment, then pushed back his sorrow and allowed himself to drift back to a happier time, when he and Mildred first met and fell in love.

"You might not believe this coming from a good lookin' guy like me, but I had to work pretty hard for Mildred to agree to our first date," he said with a glimmer of his good-natured humor breaking through his grief. "But I knew from the first time I laid eyes on her that she was the one for me."

He recalled that first encounter. It was a sunny afternoon in June at a church picnic held in Pioneer Park, a lovely grassy acreage nestled among oaks, elms, and poplars on a bluff overlooking the Mississippi River. He was twenty-one. She was a mature eighteen and was serving pies with one of her friends and some of the older ladies of the congregation. Her skin was smooth and milky, and the sun danced on her golden curls, which touched her shoulders and glistened as she busily moved back and forth. He went through the line three times—taking a slice of each variety of pie: apple, cherry, and strawberry—

before he mustered up enough courage to ask her name.

Later, she agreed to go on a walk with him along the river trail. It was there that love first began to blossom. Gutzman found himself saying things to her and revealing things about himself that he had never spoken about with anyone else before. His heart beat with joy, and he longed desperately to hold her hand. At one point during their walk, their hands began to swing out of unison and brushed against each other. He had to hold back the urge to grab her hand.

It wasn't until their third date that he finally summoned the courage to initiate that show of affection. Several weeks later she confessed that she wished he had done it on their first meeting.

"Love is a wonderful thing," said Terrell.

"Yes it is," he replied. Then, as if looking at snapshots in his mind, Gutzman spoke of the highlights of their life together. He described how nervous he was the first time he met her parents, especially the day he asked her father for her hand in marriage.

He talked of their wedding day—how it had rained early in the morning but became terribly hot and humid by the time they said their vows. At their reception, which was held at her father's farm and included only the wedding party and close friends of the family, he and his groomsmen took turns dunking their heads in a cattle trough that was filled with ice water, beer, and other beverages. As he pulled his dripping head from the icy tank, he saw his new bride from the corner of his eye. She was shaking her head in disapproval, but she had a sparkle in her eye and a small smile on her bright red lips that said, "You're a fool, but I love you anyway." It was a look she would give him many times throughout their life together; one that was as reassuring and comforting to him as the air he breathed.

Gutzman also spoke of the utter joy he felt when the doctor told him that he was the father of a healthy baby boy. There were complications during the labor, and he'd spent a long fitful night worrying and praying that Mildred and the baby would be fine. While the delivery was a success, she experienced internal problems that resulted in an emergency surgery, leaving her unable to become pregnant again.

So he and Mildred poured every ounce of love they had into their son, Frederick. She coddled and nurtured him as an infant, and as he grew, taught him manners and how to appreciate the finer things in life. He taught him how to run and throw, and hunt and fish and farm. Although the farm demanded much of their time, they always set aside Sunday as their day to be together, to rest and relax and enjoy each other's company.

⌘⌘⌘

Jenkins marveled at the stories Terrell told about Gutzman and found himself feeling melancholy over a man he didn't know.

"I understand their son, Frederick, died in Vietnam," he asked, wanting to learn more.

"Yes he did," answered Terrell. "He was a hero, so the townsfolk say. He was a helicopter pilot and risked his life flying an entire squad from behind enemy lines. After dropping them to safety he went back for more troops but was shot down. Alfred rarely discussed this. I know it hurt him deeply, but I also know he was proud of his son's valor."

Terrell and Jenkins sat in silence, pondering their conversation.

Then Terrell perked up. "Now I remember one of the most memorable things Gutzman said to me on the day of Mildred's death. As we were talking, I was amazed at how much affection he had for her and how it came through in his voice as he told me their life's story," said Terrell. "I could tell he loved her deeply. But it wasn't until he began to talk about their dreams of travel and retirement that he really got choked up. And then he said these words that I think truly embody the love he had for her. He said: 'She was my bride, and I loved her so. Her death is very difficult for me to bear. I can't imagine waking up tomorrow and not having her here. She made my life complete.'"

Jenkins looked at Terrell and nodded sympathetically. "That must have been hard to hear."

"It sure was. However, that day was also the first time I saw the deep inner strength of this man. There were many times I saw that strength give comfort and hope to others."

Jenkins listened to Terrell recount stories of Gutzman for over an hour, asking brief questions here and there, but mostly just absorbing the details of the man's life. Finally, they were interrupted by a knock on the door of his study. Standing outside was a Hispanic man with his wife and three children. This family was one of a growing number of migrant Hispanic families who had come to Marquette for the summer to work in the sweetcorn fields and at the canning plant. Jenkins wondered if they were there to ask for money.

Terrell greeted them warmly. *"Buenas días señor, señorita,"* he said, while smiling at the children and patting the youngest one on the head. *"¿Como estás?"*

When the conversation continued in Spanish, Jenkins was amazed at Terrell's fluency. Terrell invited them in, asked them to be seated, then turned to Jenkins.

"I'm sorry, but we have an appointment."

"Of course. Thank you for your time. You've been a big help," he said, looking him in the eyes and then glancing at the family, who were all seateld and smiling up at him, their bright teeth glowing through sun-darkened lips.

Terrell walked him to the door and encouraged him to attend the funeral on Monday. Jenkins felt odd about the invitation and the thought of attending but silently wondered if

60

he should go. The two shook hands and parted ways.

Jenkins walked through a long, dark hallway, down a short flight of steps, and out into the bright sunshine. His stomach growled as he crossed the street to his bike. He reluctantly looked at his watch because he knew he had missed the beginning of the game and that by this time the Twins would be deep into the mid-innings. He pulled out his cell phone, which he had turned off in Terrell's office, and pushed a speed-dial number, hoping his friend wouldn't answer, but he did.

"Matt, it's me."

"Where are ya, man? You're missing the game," he said in a disturbed tone, nearly shouting to be heard over the roar of the crowd. "I can't believe you're not here. What gives?"

"Oh, it's a long story. I'm gonna grab something to eat and then head on up. Where ya gonna be?"

"I don't know. We'll probably go to Stub and Herbs first, like always."

"Great. I'll call you when I get to the Cities and meet you there."

"Okay, dude. I'll see you when I see you," he said, sounding upset, yet preoccupied.

Jenkins pressed a key to disconnect, then hit another speed-dial number.

6

Rachel Collins had just finished mixing a batch of potato salad that she'd made from scratch in her sister's farmhouse kitchen when she heard the muffled ring of her cell phone from inside her purse. Grabbing a dishtowel from the refrigerator door handle, she wiped away some of the creamy yellow sauce from her knuckles. Reaching into her purse, she fished around until she pulled out the phone, now on its fourth ring.

"Hello," she said softly.

"Rach, this is John. Whatcha doin'?"

"Well, to be honest, I just got done mixing some potato salad. We're having a barbeque tonight."

"Oh, I forgot. Sorry."

"No, that's fine. What are you doing? Are you in the Cities?"

"No, I got tied up. Missed the game even, but I plan to make tomorrow's."

"Really?" she said, pausing. "Do you need something?"

"No, I was just hungry and thought I'd grab a bite to eat before heading out. I was gonna see if you wanted to join me. But I guess you're busy."

Rachel was surprised and somewhat flattered at his invitation. Although the two often ate lunch together, they rarely socialized outside of work. And while there were many things about Jenkins that irritated her—such as his condescending attitude toward Marquette, the fact he rarely looked her in the eyes when speaking, or how he preferred to talk mostly about himself during conversations— she still found herself attracted to him. He had a rugged handsomeness and a self-confident air, and he was always cracking jokes....

"Oh, that would have been fun," she said, trying not to sound too excited. "But we've had this planned for some time. Hey, you should join us. I'm sure Dan and Sue won't mind."

"No, I don't want to intrude. I'll just—"

She cut him off midsentence. "Hang on. I'll ask Sue."

Sue was more than happy to approve the invitation. Having observed John Jenkins and Rachel together a handful of times, she could see the way her sister felt about him, and because of that she wanted to get to know him better.

Sue had run into Jenkins once at the Corner Cupboard and had seen him a few other times when she stopped in at the *Messenger* office to deliver something to Rachel, but they had never shared more than casual conversation. It was about time, and tonight looked like a perfect night.

Rachel's voice came back on the phone a minute later. "Sue says it's fine. She'd love to have you over. I told her you're going to Minneapolis tonight, so you'd just be staying for supper. Come on over. You know where she lives, right?"

While Jenkins didn't relish the thought of having supper with a big group tonight—Rachel's sister, brother-in-law, and their three kids—he also didn't like the idea of eating alone, so he agreed. He told himself it would be quicker and easier to eat there before leaving town, plus it was on his way.

"Sure. Just north of town, right?"

"Yeah, big white house on the west side of the road. Where are you now?"

"Still in town. I'll be there in a little bit."

"Great. See you then," she said.

After hanging up the phone, Rachel was flushed with excitement. Sue couldn't help but grin at her sister as she rushed to the bathroom to fix her hair and makeup.

⌘⌘⌘

Jenkins passed the city limits sign and immediately noticed a white farmhouse on the east side of the road. Then he recalled his conversation with his boss the day before: *"His name is Alfred Gutzman, and he owned the farmstead just north of town, past the city limits."* Those words swirled around in his mind as he drove by the farm, taking a long look while piecing together the tragedies that haunted that place: the tornado, the death of a child, the death of a spouse. He averted his eyes back to the road, then peered into his rearview mirror for another glimpse. He turned his head to see the farm one last time, then focused his attention back on the road so he wouldn't miss the turn to Rachel's sister's house, which he could now see, less than a quarter mile down the road.

⌘⌘⌘

The gravel popped and snapped under the tires of Jenkins' motorcycle as he turned off the highway and onto the driveway that stretched three hundred yards straightaway to a white, two-story farmhouse. The lane was surrounded by a field bursting forth with tiny lime-green corn plants that were several inches high and just beginning to form their skinny, pointed leaves. As he followed the driveway, he approached a freshly mowed lawn, which looked healthy from the highway but at closer inspection was a mixture of grass, crab grass, dandelions, and other assorted weeds.

The bright white house with black shutters on the front windows looked attractive and well-kept. Next to it was a two-vehicle garage, unattached and seemingly only a few years old. Behind it was a large white barn with a fenced livestock corral, a silo, machine shed, and two other small buildings. The yard was filled with towering, magnificent oak trees that provided shade for much of the house and yard. They lined the southern boundary of the property like giant palace pillars and were scattered throughout the yard in no particular pattern, testifying that they had roots there long before the homestead was established.

Rachel appeared as soon as he neared the house, letting the screen door slam with a loud slap behind her. Her brother-in-law was tending to a mound of hot, glowing coals in a large Weber grill near the garage, and his three kids—Aaron, Cody, and Andrew, ages two to seven—were playing on a nearby wooden swing set structure, complete with three swings, a small enclosed platform, and a faded yellow slide.

Jenkins stopped near the back door, revved his engine slightly, then shut off the machine, with Rachel's and Dan's eyes upon him. Sue came out of the house, her left hand gently guiding the screen door shut behind her, her right hand carrying a plate stacked three-high with raw hamburger patties.

"I hope you're hungry because we've got a lot of burgers here," she said, looking at Jenkins and motioning at the plate. She smiled at him and kept walking toward her husband.

Dan also smiled at him and nodded upward to acknowledge him, then fixed his eyes on Sue, who was reaching out to hand him the plate. He took it from her, raised the plate, and smiled again. Then he and Sue faced the grill and started to lay the burgers on the hot metal grate, with each patty sizzling as it was added.

"I guess you found it okay," Rachel said.

"Yeah, good memory." Jenkins had been to the farm one time before, just a few days after he arrived in town. Rachel's car was in the shop so he had given her a ride to the farm after work. He had sped the entire way on purpose, making frequent accelerated bursts that made her clutch him tightly at the waist to keep from falling off. It was the first and last time she had ridden on his motorcycle.

"Are you hungry?"

"Yeah, I am."

"Well, supper is almost ready. All we have to do is grill the burgers. I'll finish getting the fixin's," she said and turned toward the house.

"Can I help?"

"No, I can get it."

He watched her enter the house, again slamming the screen door behind her, and then turned toward Dan and Sue, feeling uncomfortable and wishing Rachel had asked for his help. He walked over to them.

"Hi again. Need any help?"

"No, we're fine," said Sue.

"Yeah, go ahead and grab a beer from the cooler," Dan said, pointing to a red and white plastic cooler that was sitting between two of four green hard plastic lawn chairs that were placed in a semi-circle between the grill and a picnic table that was covered with a red and white checkered table cloth.

"We have pop in there, too," Sue added. "And wine coolers in the house."

"Thanks," he said as he walked over to the cooler, popped its lid, and grabbed a bottle of Budweiser half buried in small chunks of ice. He closed the lid, unscrewed the bottle cap, and looked around for a trash bag. Not seeing one, he slid the cap in his pocket and sat down. He immediately noticed the refreshing dip in temperature provided by the shade of a nearby oak tree. He took one sip of his beer and was suddenly surrounded in a whirlwind of excitement.

"Hey. Wanna play ball?" chimed Aaron, the oldest and most vociferous of the children who ruled the yard. He had a leather ball glove on his left hand and was tossing a darkened baseball in and out of it as he waited for a response. His two younger brothers were shoulder-to-shoulder, standing slightly behind him, with wide eyes that said, "Yeah, let's play."

"Honey, I think Mr. Jenkins would prefer to just relax," their mother yelled from a distance. "Go along and play," she told them.

"Oh, Mom. We need someone to pitch to us. I want to hit for once," the eldest cried back, while his siblings droned in unison, "Yeaaaah."

"No, kids. Besides, it's time to eat. Run in and wash your hands."

"Yeah, hangerberths," lisped Andrew, the youngest, as the three raced for the house.

Rachel met them at the door as she was coming out with a tray filled with sliced tomatoes, onions, pickles, ketchup and mustard, and a bowl of potato salad. Under her right arm was a bag of potato chips. She held the door open with her foot to let the youngsters scamper through, then let it bang shut. Jenkins jumped up to help her with her load.

"Thanks," she said as he grabbed the tray from her and walked it over to the picnic table.

"Rachel, can you get some root beer and pour it for the kids, please?" Sue asked.

"Sure." Rachel then asked Jenkins to get three cans of root beer from the cooler as she began to place paper plates, plastic eating utensils, Styrofoam cups, and napkins around the table.

Soon the entire family converged on the table and sat down. Grace was said, and plates were passed. The men took the biggest burgers and loaded them up with all available condiments and took huge scoops of potato salad and large handfuls of chips, while the women took the smaller patties and fixed the smallest ones for the children. Few words were said as the meal was enjoyed in a gentle breeze under the late afternoon sun. Soon the kids scampered off to more games of baseball and tag, and Sue and Rachel cleared the table while Dan and John retreated to the lawn chairs.

"Have another?" Dan said while retrieving himself a beer.

"Sure," Jenkins replied, taking the bottle from him. "You have a nice place here. Lived here long?"

"My entire life. My great grandfather built this house in 1899, and our family has worked this farm ever since. I took over from my dad a few years ago."

"Wow, you've never lived anywhere else?" Jenkins asked, finding it hard to imagine the thought of it. Jenkins' family was always on the move, usually because they were upgrading to a larger, more luxurious home. Although he always lived in a suburb of Minneapolis, he'd never lived in one house for more than four years, about the time it took for his father to get another promotion.

"Nope. I've never lived anywhere else, except for college. Had a few fun years, but I eventually came back home. This place is in my blood, I guess," he said as Sue and Rachel returned with opened wine coolers and took a seat beside them.

"What's it like growing up on a farm?" asked Jenkins.

"It's a good life. Plain and simple, but good. There's something very rewarding about makin' your livin' off the land. It's not for everyone, that's for sure. It takes a lot of faith and perseverance."

"Yeah, and a lot of hard work for little pay," jibbed Sue as she smiled at her husband, and the two shared a small laugh.

"But don't you get your winters off?" said Jenkins.

"Winters off?" Dan snapped back. "You city boys just don't

know what it takes to put the meat and potatoes on the table, do ya?"

Jenkins realized he'd struck a nerve.

"Dan!" Sue said sharply. "He didn't mean anything by it."

"John, let me tell you what life is really like on a farm," he said, ignoring his wife's plea and eager to enlighten his guest. "Most every day starts at or before the sun comes up. Whoever came up with the phrase 24-7 must have been talkin' about farmers, because we don't get too many nights and weekends off. There are fields to till and plant in the spring. And if the good Lord is smilin' on us, he lets us in the fields early so we can get the crops in.

"But most years the weather doesn't cooperate and we get in late, which means some of our poorer fields won't produce as well. Then I'm busy sprayin', diggin' drain tile, and pickin' rocks from the fields to make sure my crops have the best chance to grow. When harvest time comes, I'm in the fields from sun-up to ten or eleven at night. Then I drag my tired butt into bed, only to wake up the next morning and do it all over again. And when I've had about all I can take, it's finally time to haul my crops to the elevator and see if I'll make enough to cover costs for another year's worth of expenses of runnin' a farm and raising a family.

"And the winters? Yeah, they might be a little slower, but that's when we fix our machinery, catch up on several months of overdue paperwork and bills, and begin plannin' for another season. Most years it's fine and we do okay, but if we have a really wet spring or a really dry summer, things can get tight. It doesn't take long to incur a lot of debt to help cover losses from year to year. We're a small business, John, and we have fixed expenses just like every other small business does. The only difference is that we have to wait until harvest time to see if we can cover those expenses."

"I'm sorry. I didn't mean to offend you. I guess I've never

given it much thought. It sounds like a tricky business."

"It is," Dan replied, now cooling off. "To be honest, there are many days when I'm in the fields that I wonder why I do this. I could make a lot more money workin' an eight-to-five somewhere, like you. But, like I said, the land gets in your blood and under your nails. There's a satisfaction that comes from this way of life that I don't think you can find anywhere else, and that's what I just can't give up. This farm is my home, and our neighbors are like my family. I wouldn't trade 'em for the world."

Jenkins conceded the debate and quickly switched topics, not wanting to appear ungrateful to his hosts for their hospitality. "So you're pretty close to your neighbors, huh?" he asked, looking to the southeast and in the direction of the Gutzman farm. "I'm sure you've heard about Alfred Gutzman?"

"Yes, we have," said Dan, sadly.

"Were you close to him?"

"Yeah, I knew him very well. My grandfather sold him that farm," he said, pointing toward it. "My dad and Al's son were close friends and served together in Vietnam. My dad was lucky enough to come home. His son wasn't. Alfred Gutzman was a very respectable man—a hard worker, an honest man who went out of his way to help others. Many times he helped us get our crops in or out of the field when we had machinery trouble, and he never expected anything in return for it. It's unfortunate he passed away, but he had a good, long life. He's happier now."

"Yeah, he helped us out of a jam once, didn't he, honey?" said Sue with a big silly grin. "Go ahead, tell him the story. We need a good laugh."

Dan laughed out loud in acknowledgement and began to tell the story....

⌘⌘⌘

"Baby, I think you've had too much to drink. Let me drive," pleaded Sue in a high-pitched voice, herself a little tipsy. She and Dan had spent the night at Joe's Bar drinking beer and a few shots of whiskey with some high school friends, who were all home from separate colleges for the homecoming football game.

"No way. I'm fine," he slurred.

"Come on. Let me drive."

"Get in. I'm drivin'."

Sue shrugged, opened the passenger door of his pickup, stepped onto the running board, and pulled herself into the cab, her curly hair brushing the frame as she slid through.

Dan was already in the driver's seat, digging deep into the pockets of his faded jeans for his keys. He pulled them out and stared hard at them as he spun them around the ring, one by one, until he found the key he needed. As he fumbled to put it into the ignition, he dropped the keys to the floor, jingling as they hit the floor mat. When he reached down to pick them up, he leaned onto the steering wheel, producing a horn blast that blared loudly into the night. Quickly he removed his arm and started to laugh, as did Sue. He finally matched the key with the ignition and started the engine.

"Tired?" he said as he regarded her with a mischievous look.

She didn't say a word but her coy grin let him know that she would take part in his obvious romantic scheme.

Dan drove slowly out of town, taking special precaution to make a complete stop at each stop sign and to signal every turn. At the edge of town, past the Ford dealership, a gravel road jutted off the highway to the east and followed a winding path northward along the river for six miles until it looped back to the west and reconnected with the same highway. It was a narrow, minimum maintenance road, which meant the county did little for its upkeep. In the spring, workers would fill the worst ruts and potholes with gravel and grade them out smooth, but that was the extent of it. In the winter, they did not plow it, which left it impassable for months at a time. The county's abandonment of the road was to the pleasure of high school students and young adults in their early twenties, who would use it for a place to drink and engage in affectionate behavior that they could not do at home for fear of being caught by their parents.

Once Dan turned onto the river road, he accelerated swiftly, knowing he was safe from the law since they rarely patrolled the road. It was dark and quiet, and there wasn't another vehicle in sight, so he pulled into the first field approach he saw, his heart racing with excitement for what was about to take place.

The black dirt leading to the field was now a mass of gooey mud since it had been raining most of the week. As Dan turned sharply into the approach, he entered it too fast, causing the truck tires to sink into the thick mud. Knowing they were in danger of being helplessly stuck, he quickly shifted to reverse and prayed his rear wheels would find enough solid ground to get them out of the predicament. They didn't, but spun freely, sending mud splattering into the road behind them. In his anger and frustration, he beat the dashboard three times, then quickly shifted between forward and reverse in an attempt to rock the vehicle free. That, too, was unsuccessful. More cursing and abuse of the dashboard followed...and this time the windshield as well.

Sue started to cry.

"Quiet!" he shouted. "I'll get us out of this."

He opened the door and stepped out, sinking to his ankles in the deep mud.

"Move over," he demanded, which she did, sliding swiftly from her side of the cab to his and inching forward so her feet could reach the pedals. "Put it in reverse, and when I say go, hit the gas."

As he walked to the front of the truck, the mud sucked his penny-loafer from his left foot. He hopped on his right leg as he fished around for his shoe with his toes, and when he finally found it he pushed his foot deep into it and pulled it free by pointing his toes upward. He got to the front of the truck, the headlights blinding him, braced his legs in a staggered stance, and barked out his command.

Sue shifted to reverse and thrust her right foot hard at the gas pedal, causing the engine to rev loudly and the wheels to spin madly. The action moved the truck just enough to make Dan lose his balance, causing him to slip and fall, his forehead grazing the bumper before he landed into the cool, wet goo. Sue was looking over her shoulder, her foot now fully depressing the gas pedal, the tires still spinning wildly, burying the truck deeper and deeper into the mud.

Dan jumped up, the complete right side of his face dripping with thick, black mud, and shouted, "Stop!"

Sue whipped her head around, pulled her foot from the gas pedal, and peered through the windshield and into the headlight beam. She shifted to park and stared at him for a moment, then started to laugh uncontrollably. After that momentary outburst, she turned off the engine and began to cry again.

Just then Dan could hear the sputter of a tractor making its way along the southern boundary of the field. Its lone headlight shone dimly in the night. His first reaction was to grab Sue and run and hide, but he knew that was a foolish plan.

"Turn off the lights," he said quietly, standing there covered with mud, as the tractor slowly made its way toward them.

"Looks like you're having a bit of trouble there, son," said a voice from behind the tractor's headlamp.

"Mr. Gutzman. Is that you?"

"Sure is, Danny. You're a mess. Takin' the long way home, I see," he said as he climbed off his tractor, his high black rubber boots keeping the mud from his pant legs.

He walked over to the truck. "Sue," said Gutzman, looking very stern, "I don't think your mama would approve of you being out this late. Is she expecting you soon?"

Sue began to weep again, nodded in affirmation, and slid down in the seat in embarrassment.

Gutzman looked at Dan, who also averted his eyes in embarrassment, and then trudged back to his tractor. He climbed on, drove it behind the truck and dismounted, while grabbing a thick, rusty chain.

"Hook it to the axle, Danny. I don't want to get dirty," he said as he fastened the other end to the back of his tractor. "Now get in, and let's get you out of here."

⌘⌘⌘

Rachel had tears in her eyes from laughter as Dan told the story.

"You never told me that one, sis," she said to Sue, who had told her most of her secrets while growing up.

"I didn't want that one to get back to Dad," Sue admitted. "Plus, I went back to college the next day and forgot all about it."

"How about you?" Jenkins asked Dan. "Did you get busted? Did Gutzman tell your parents?"

"No, that's the kicker. He made me promise to return to his house after I dropped off Sue, which I did. He let me shower and his wife brewed me a pot of coffee. She told me to drink the entire pot and then went to bed while Al went outside and hosed down my truck. And he never told my old man, at least not that I'm aware of."

Sue's smile faded, and tiny bittersweet tears moistened her eyes. "Yeah, he never told anyone about that night, but he always had a special little glimmer in his eye for me every time I saw him. He was such a nice man. I'm gonna miss him."

7

Although the guilt of missing the Twins game with his friends was weighing heavily on him, Jenkins knew the moment he reached the highway that he had one more stop to make before heading to the Twin Cities. Turning right and traveling south toward Marquette, he quickly throttled-up to the posted speed limit and then released his grip, the whine of the engine subsiding as he decreased his speed and made a left-hand turn into the driveway of the Gutzman farm. Self-conscious of what he was doing, he peered behind him to see if there were any other motorists on the road who might see him enter the property.

The sun was starting to melt into the horizon as he drove down the long driveway and maneuvered his bike between a towering white wooden barn and a low silver metal machine shed so that he was fully out of sight of the highway. For a reason he couldn't explain, he had an unusual desire to walk around this farmstead and get a feel for the place that Alfred Gutzman called home. He swung his right leg over the bike, dropped the kickstand, and slid the key into his right pocket. Digging both hands deep into the front pockets of his faded blue jeans, he admired the landscape. He'd never before appreciated the simplistic beauty of rural land but now couldn't help but admire it as dusk splashed an amber hue across the fields and lawn and created dark silhouettes out of the trees and outbuildings.

As he walked slowly around the yard and over to the house, he took every precaution to stay out of sight from the passing traffic on the highway, and he tried to imagine the tornado that had besieged this place and the family that lived here. He looked around for remnants of its destruction but could find none. The fields looked like every other field he'd ever seen, the house seemed in order, and even the largest and most mature trees looked normal.

I wonder..., he thought as he stepped up onto the concrete landing of the back door of the faded white farmhouse and reached out for the handle. He turned the knob slowly and, to his surprise, the door clicked open. Startled, he quickly pulled it shut, stretched his head around the corner of the house, and shot a glance toward the highway, which was quiet. He looked over to his motorcycle, reassured himself that it was well concealed, and again turned the door handle. This time he swung the door halfway open, slid through the crack, and shut it quietly behind him.

He turned around and found himself in the kitchen. The sunlight coming in from the window over the white porcelain sink was doing its best to illuminate the room, yet it was still dim inside. The kitchen was large but contained few furnishings, including a small wooden table with two spindle-backed chairs and a small desk that had on it a phone, a phonebook, and various pieces of mail and other papers.

He crept across the tan-checkered linoleum floor to the refrigerator and opened it. It was sparsely stocked with milk, eggs, cheese, bologna and salami, potatoes, onions and apples, and two clear plastic containers holding what appeared to be leftovers. In the freezer was a half gallon of maple nut ice cream, a few bags of frozen vegetables, and several packages of meat, all wrapped in white butcher shop paper and labeled with a red stamp. As he closed the door, he wondered what would become of this food. *Who's gonna clean this stuff out before it rots?* he thought. *And what's gonna happen to this house and all that's in it?*

From the kitchen he walked through a wide opening that flowed into the living room. It was modestly decorated with one large brown tweed sofa, a wooden rocking chair, a tan E-Z chair, two mahogany end tables with matching brass lamps, and a wooden entertainment center that housed a small TV and an old stereo system that had a radio, cassette, and record player. As he scanned the room he noticed the long, dark pleated drapes that hung from ceiling to floor on both sides of a large picture window that looked to the west, and a few pieces of inexpensive art on the walls.

Next to an embroidered wall hanging that read, *As for me and my house, we will serve the Lord,* was a framed photo that caught his attention: a family portrait. Jenkins hurriedly walked over to the photo and fixed his gaze upon it. He could tell it had been taken in the '60s by the clothing of the man, woman, and young man in it, and he was deeply shocked by what he saw. The stranger he'd been hearing about for the past two days suddenly had a face, and it was smiling directly back at him. The Alfred Gutzman he saw in the photograph was a handsome, well-groomed man. He was wearing a dark navy blue suit and skinny blue tie. His short hair was greased back and combed from right to left across his scalp. His eyes were steel blue, his nose long and slender, and his cleft chin protruded beneath a broad toothy smile. For several minutes, Jenkins closely examined each of his features, often looking deeply into his eyes, as if searching for his soul.

"Wow, so that's you, huh?" he whispered out loud, and then turned his eyes toward Gutzman's wife. She was wearing a light blue dress that complemented her full-bodied, middle-aged figure. Her black hair was pulled back into a high bun and had streaks of gray running through it, but her dark brown eyes sparkled with life. She was sitting between Alfred and their son, who were both standing. The young man, who was wearing light blue polyester pants and a white shirt and blue tie, was also handsome and held himself in a proud, confident manner. He had an Ivy-League crewcut, short in the back but slightly longer on the top, and many of the same rugged features of his father.

The three looked so happy that Jenkins smiled...until he remembered the fate of the woman and young son. Then he felt a twinge of sadness deep in the center of his stomach. He recalled his own family's portrait, taken his senior year; one that still hung above the fireplace in his father's house. It too had just three people in it—him, his father, and his stepmother. They were all dressed in expensive clothing, looking very prim and proper. The stuffy portrait was a sharp contrast to the one he was now viewing.

Was this family really happy, or is it just a facade? he wondered. He looked more closely at each person again and noticed how content and comfortable they appeared, and how natural they looked with each other. *Maybe they knew their time would be cut short, so they made the most of it,* he pondered, but quickly realized the absurdity of the statement. *How could they? Maybe they actually were a happy family.*

Jenkins headed down a hallway, grabbed the smooth, dark cone of the banister, and guided himself around it as he began to climb the staircase to the second story of the home. Once upstairs he could see a bathroom and the doors to three rooms, only one of which was closed. In the hallway was a cedar chest covered with a blue and beige quilt, checkered with a repeating pattern. He peeked into the bathroom and saw one towel neatly folded over a bar on the shower door and a solitary toothbrush in a hard plastic cup by the sink. He moved on to the next room and noticed that there wasn't much in it except for a single bed and a chest of drawers. Jenkins assumed it was a spare bedroom that got little use.

The door to the neighboring room was closed so he gripped the knob, turned it, and swung it open. His first glance into the

79

room told him that it was Frederick's room. Inside was a single bed with a burgundy bedspread and one dresser. On the dresser were a few athletic trophies, a small transistor radio, a framed photograph of a pretty teenage girl, a pocketknife and a change dish filled with only silver coins. The walls were covered with posters of vintage rock 'n' roll groups: the Beatles, the Rolling Stones, and Simon & Garfunkel.

He took a closer look at the girl in the photograph, admired her beauty, and wondered who she was. After walking out of that room, he closed the door behind him, making sure it clasped shut. There were over thirty years of memories locked up in that room, and he didn't want to be the one to let them out.

Moving down the hall he came to the master bedroom. The room was somewhat larger than the other two and housed a queen-size bed, a large mirrored bureau, a small writing desk, and a large wardrobe closet. The only artwork on the walls was a paper copy of the twenty-third Psalm shellacked on a shiny slab of walnut, a wooden cross, and a handful of photographs of the family members at various stages in their lives. He opened the closet door and saw one row of hanging clothes. The right half of the rack held one dark navy blue suit, one gray suit, two white pressed and starched dress shirts, and several casual shirts, mostly flannel and denim in different degrees of wear. The left side of the rack held only blue jeans and overalls. On the floor was one pair of highly shined black dress shoes and two pairs of work boots, one pair relatively new and the other one well-worn.

Closing the closet, he walked past the bureau and caught a shadow of movement out of the corner of his eye. It alarmed him at first and then he quickly realized that it was his own reflection that he saw. He turned toward the mirror, looked into his own eyes and said to himself, *What am I doing here? I must be crazy. I've got to get out of here before I get busted.* But then, while still gazing into the mirror, he noticed an open spiral notebook on the desk behind him, with a ballpoint pen resting on top of the right-hand page. Curious, he walked over and took a look. The page was half filled with cursive writing and dated at the top.

May 29, 2006

It's been over twenty years, yet the magnitude of this day still weighs heavy on my heart. I found it difficult to retire last night and probably didn't get to sleep until 3 a.m., and even then I tossed and turned, reliving the terrible hours of that day. Mildred was a wonderful woman, and I still miss her deeply and grieve the fact that our time together was cut short. Sometimes I still wonder why God took her and Frederick from me, but then I know they are in a much better place.

Today I will visit their graves and try to remember only the joy and laughter that filled the time we shared together. I will try not to mourn. I did enough of that last night. I will remember the good times, her smile, her strength, her wit and courage. It is a beautiful morning, the sun is shining, the birds are singing, and the temperature is very agreeable. I believe I will walk to the cemetery today. I'm sure the exercise will do me good and help clear my mind and release me from this mournful stupor.

Jenkins reread the passage again in great amazement to reaffirm what he had discovered.

Incredible. A journal. He died on the same day as his wife, he thought as he grabbed the left side of the notebook and flipped it over to view its cover. It was a simple red spiral notebook, the kind that most high school and college students use to take notes for their classes. There was nothing written on the front cover except for the date: *October 2005*. Jenkins fanned the pages with his thumb, starting with the back pages, then stopped at a random spot and read the entry.

April 12, 2006

It looks as if this early spring will hold. The snow has been completely melted for nearly three weeks, and we've had warm temperatures and steady rains every few days since then. The soil looks like black gold, and I can smell its pungent aroma from my back porch. I've noticed my neighbors are already out preparing for the busy planting season. It will be here any day. I envy them because I know what they are thinking — that maybe this is the year that they get their crops in early and that they will reap a bumper crop at harvest.

As I think back over the years I can recall only a handful of times that we had a spring like the one we're having. It was terribly exciting—the thought of what the year might bring, and what it did bring. It's times like these that keeps a farmer optimistic, and keeps him farming. I find it peculiar that the land still calls to me after so many years and that I still long to be out there working it, even though it has worn me out. I often have to remind myself how much work it takes to make a living by farming. Nonetheless, this looks like a good year, and I pray that it is for my neighbors.

Jenkins lifted the notebook from the desk, took it over to the bed, and sat down on the corner of the mattress closest to the west-facing window to take advantage of the incoming sunlight, which was growing dimmer by the minute. He wanted to keep reading, but the lack of light was making it difficult. He knew that if he turned on the light, though, it might be seen from the highway.

Scanning the room, he glimpsed a half-burned candle on top of the bureau. He tucked the notebook under his arm, walked over to the bureau, and opened one of the top three skinny drawers. It was filled with white handkerchiefs, folded and stacked in two rows of three. He closed the drawer and opened the one next to it. It was filled with miscellaneous items such as keys, a knife, and a pocket watch, and also had the item he was searching for—matches. He pulled them from the drawer, grabbed the candle, and walked out into the hallway, closing the door behind him.

Walking over to the guest bedroom, he closed that door, too, as well as the door to the bathroom, becoming enshrouded in darkness. He sat down on the cedar chest, folded back the quilt to expose the wood, placed the candle next to him, and then extracted a small wooden match from the box and struck it briskly on the starter panel. He put the flame to the wick and watched the dark hallway brighten enough to allow him to continue reading the journal.

Most of the pages were filled with small details of Gutzman's life—observations about the weather, his health, meetings he had with friends—but every so often he would use the pages to express his feelings and heal old wounds.

Jenkins skimmed through several of the entries until he came to one written on Veterans Day.

November 11, 2005

I awoke today very stiff and sore. As I got out of bed and hobbled to the kitchen for my morning cup of coffee, I remembered my plans for the day—to attend the Veterans Day service at Vets Park. I can't help but believe that many of my aches and pains are a result of the time I spent on the battlefield during WWII.

The images I saw there haunt me to this day, and I still have memories that are difficult to bear. I've only confided in a few people about my experiences there, and most of them are gone now. I will go to today's service and again hide the fact that I fought against this great country when I was a young man. It truly seems like a different life, yet when I stop and remember, it seems like it was only yesterday.

There was a time that I loved Germany, and a part of me still does. The late 1930s and early 1940s was a wonderful time to be a German. For an industrious land run by industrious people, the possibilities seemed endless for us as we grew to be a world power.

But as history has pointed out, it was built on a corrupt base. I still find it hard to believe how an entire country could get so wrapped up in such strange ideals, but it happened, and I was part of it.

I fought hard for my country and was decorated for it—something I have never spoken of to anyone else. When I deserted that country, my home, I vowed that the person I was then would stay there. It was very painful leaving, knowing I would likely never see my family again. My brother, also a soldier, died in the war, but my parents and two sisters survived the frequent bombings that I later learned took place in our small hamlet.

It took me many years before I had the courage to contact them. But, of course, they welcomed me back with open arms. However, it wasn't until I shared the horrors of what I'd seen in that concentration camp that they realized that what I had done was just and right. I told them about the day I stood by and watched two dozen Jewish men march into a shower building and get gassed to death. That was the day I stopped being a soldier and started fighting to be a man. It still sickens me to this day that my countrymen could do something so inhumane.

Today I will go to the service and honor the memory of the men, women, and children who have lost their lives in war—no matter which country they have pledged allegiance to. I know there are just wars, but at this stage of my life I find them difficult to justify.

I was very proud of Frederick's service to our country, as I know he was, but for a long time I felt that my son's death was my punishment for my actions during WWII. But I'm not sure God works that way. All I know is that he and Mildred are in a much better place now and are free from pain. I patiently wait for the day that I can join them again.

Jenkins gently closed the journal as the candlelight flickered and danced on the walls around him. He felt tired and emotionally drained from reading the journal. He rubbed his eyes and glanced at his watch, which read 9:21. He blinked his eyes hard and looked at it again. "Oh man, I've got to get goin'," he said out loud.

He blew out the candle and crept cautiously out of the house.

8

Jenkins woke up late Sunday morning, showered quickly, then raced his motorcycle to Minneapolis. He parked in a ramp near Target Field and ran the two blocks to the Will Call booth, where he picked up his ticket for the second game of the Twins' two-game series with the Brewers. Giving his ticket to a gray-haired man in a red smock, Jenkins pushed his way through the crowd to enter the ballpark. The concourse was alive with other latecomers who, like Jenkins, were also weaving toward their seats to get there before the first pitch.

As Jenkins hurried down a flight of steps to section 119, the bright sunshine and dark green grass of the ball field quickly unfolded before him. He could feel the energy of the crowd, waiting impatiently for the opening festivities to be over and for the first pitch to be thrown out so the game could begin. Players from both teams were running off the field following their warm-ups and the umpires were making their way to their assigned positions.

As he approached his seat, the PA announcer was reminding the crowd that there was "noooo smooooking at Target Field." The crowd gave its customary roar of approval while the smokers present remained stone-faced, knowing they'd be outside by the nearest gate enjoying a drag right after the game was over.

"Well, look who made it," said Matt Weber loudly, pointing toward Jenkins with a long, bony finger. He was visibly perturbed, and his eyebrows crested to punctuate his anger.

Jenkins and Weber had known each other since they were freshmen at the U. They were assigned as roommates in the dorm and had been the rare pair who actually became close friends and continued living together throughout their collegiate career. Weber, a business major who now worked as a sales representative for a national insurance firm in Minneapolis, shared many of the same interests as Jenkins, especially a love of sports.

Jenkins cocked his head to his left and flashed a sarcastic smile at Weber as he shuffled through the row to get to his seat, climbing over a half dozen people, most of whom were wearing a T-shirt or jersey with the familiar blue and red Twins logo on it. Sitting next to Weber were Tom Ashland and Corey Flemming. The four had lived together in an apartment off campus their junior and senior years. They too shared a love of sports, both watching and playing, and, like Jenkins and Weber, came from rather privileged families. As seniors, the foursome attended as many professional sporting events as their coursework allowed—be it the Vikings, Timberwolves, Wild, or Twins. Money never seemed to be an issue for any of them, and if it was, a quick call home remedied the situation.

Before Jenkins could address them, the PA announcer's voice again resonated throughout the ballpark, this time urging everyone to stand and pay tribute to the U.S.A. They stood up with the rest of the nearly 17,000 fans and listened to a high school trio beautifully harmonize its way through the national anthem, hitting the high notes perfectly. Jenkins and his friends left their Twins baseball hats on during the anthem, unlike most of the older men in the crowd who removed theirs out of respect and placed them over their hearts.

"Man, where ya been? I was trying to get ahold of you all last night and this morning. How come you turned off your cell?" asked Weber as they were sitting down.

"Oh man, it's a long story."

"What could be more important than a Twins game on a Saturday afternoon in June?"

"I just got wrapped up on a story, sorry."

"I thought all you had to do was take pictures at some stupid little parade?"

Ashland and Flemming watched the players take the field but had their ears tuned to the spat taking place next to them. Both were accustomed to the verbal bantering that often took place between Jenkins and Weber. Knowing them to be strong-willed and opinionated individuals, they waited patiently to enter the conversation.

"I did, but something else came up," replied Jenkins, irritated with the interrogation.

He wasn't in the mood to explain himself and wanted only to get lost in the action of the game. He hadn't slept well the night before because he kept thinking about Gutzman and the time he spent in his house. Although he slept in his own comfortable bed, he tossed and turned all night long and had bizarre dreams. The only ones he could partially recall involved him driving his motorcycle through the mud and another about him eating dinner in a farmhouse that was filled with people he didn't know.

"Well, what was it?" Weber demanded.

"Do you really want to know?" said Jenkins as a fly ball cracked off the end of a Brewer's bat and sped toward their seats, which were just to the left of the backstop net. Looking like a mammoth, multi-tentacled monster, the crowd, including their friends, sprung to their feet, raising their arms high in the air to catch the foul ball. Jenkins and Weber remained seated, instinctively crouching down and putting their arms over their heads to shield themselves.

That action brought a faint smile to both of them. They were alike in so many ways. *Maybe that's why we get on each other's nerves,* Jenkins thought.

"Well, you're gonna think I'm crazy, but I'm working on an obituary about this old farmer and I can't get him off of my mind. It's been one strange turn of events after another since I got the assignment on Friday. It seems as if everywhere I turn, I run into someone who has something to say about this guy."

"You're jokin', right?" said Weber as he mulled over the thought and jabbed Ashland in the side with his elbow. "Hey, Johnny blew us off yesterday to write an obituary."

He, Flemming, and Ashland laughed simultaneously, bumping shoulders to animate their mockery.

"Johnny, you've hit the big time. Looks like that degree is payin' off," quipped Ashland.

Although it was common, maybe even expected, for these four to rib each other at every possible opportunity, the remark annoyed Jenkins. Rather than perpetuating the situation he turned his attention to an overweight vendor who was breathing heavily and sweating profusely as he lugged a cooler of beer up the nearby flight of steps. Jenkins reached into his back pocket and pulled out his brown leather wallet. He opened it, retrieved a $20 bill, and held it high in the air for the vendor to see.

"Who wants one?" he said, looking back over his shoulder toward his friends.

"It's about time," crowed Weber.

"Make it a round," commanded Ashland.

Jenkins held up four fingers. The vendor stopped, put down his case, and bellowed out the amount while confirming nonverbally that they wanted regular over light beer. Jenkins grabbed another $5 and passed the money through the crowd. Once it reached the vendor, he quickly pocketed it, grabbed a dollar in change and passed it back through the crowd with the first bottle, followed quickly by the other three. Jenkins watched as the four beers bounced back toward him and relayed all but the last one to his friends.

The Twins had acquired a new pitcher in the off-season, and he looked promising. He was starting today and was the topic of much of their early conversation. The team had been inconsistent the past few years but showed a spark of hope the previous fall in its run for the American League Central title, although coming up short. The four friends spent much of the game spouting off one statistic after another as the players rotated through the lineup.

During the seventh inning stretch Jenkins and his friends filed through the crowd and found the men's room. By this time each had paid for a round of beer, which made the end of the sixth inning slightly uncomfortable for them all.

The Twins had a commanding lead at this point, topping the Brewers 5-2, so they decided to join the mob of hungry fans and get in line for another beer and a huge quarter-pound hot dog, which they loaded up with ketchup, mustard, onions, and relish at the condiment bar.

The count was 3-1 on the third batter in the lineup by the time they returned to their seats and sat down, each putting his beer in the seat's cup holder and his hot dog in his lap. Little was said as they devoured their food, washing down every other bite with long swallows of cold beer.

"Where we goin' after the game?" Weber finally said, wiping ketchup from his upper lip while balling up his foil hot dog wrapper and tossing it on the floor.

"Wanna go to Huberts?" asked Ashland.

"Naw. Too many married women. How about Stub and Herbs," replied Flemming, referring to the popular campus bar.

"Sounds good to me. What do ya think, Johnny?" asked Weber.

"Let's do it."

⌘⌘⌘

Traffic was extremely congested after the game, so it took Jenkins over twenty minutes to travel the handful of miles from the ballpark to the bar and another five minutes snaking around side streets and alleys to find a parking spot. By the time he met his friends at the entrance of Stub and Herbs, located in the heart of the university's campus town, the bar was already teeming with an eclectic mix of students and alumni. The four entered and meandered their way to the bar, looking to Weber for their next round. Knowing it was his turn to buy the next round of drinks, he already had his money in hand and waved it in the air to get the bartender's attention. While he waited impatiently for the drinks, Jenkins and his other two friends squeezed into a nearby nook of the bar.

Weber finally joined the group and doled out the beverages, with each taking a drink as soon as he received his beer. It was too loud to talk, so they stood tall, trying to look cool, and scanned the room for pretty girls, pointing out their finds to each other. While Jenkins normally took part in this post-game ogling ritual, he found himself getting annoyed with the intolerable crowd and the loudness of the place. His thoughts turned to Marquette and, for the first time since he moved there, he began to appreciate the sensibility of the quiet little town. After fifteen minutes, he made up his mind to leave and chugged down his last swallow of his beer.

"I've got to get going," he said, setting his bottle on a nearby rail.

"What? We just got here! What's up with you this weekend?" shouted Weber.

"Hey, I've got a long drive and a busy week ahead of me."

"So when has that ever stopped you?"

Weber was probably the closest friend Jenkins ever had, yet he was still uncomfortable talking to him about the true reason that he was out of sorts. The past few days had made an impact on him that even he didn't fully understand. All he knew was that for some strange reason he felt compelled to get back to Marquette, away from the metropolitan area that he had always loved and thrived upon.

Undeterred by the remark, Jenkins slapped his friend on the back as the other two looked at him quizzically. "Hey, I promised my old man I'd stop by today. I'll be back next weekend. I'll give you a call."

⌘⌘⌘

Jenkins could feel the effects of the beer so he drove his motorcycle cautiously to his father's home in Eden Prairie, just twenty minutes away. It was his intention to stop in, say hello, chat over one or two cups of coffee or iced tea, and be on the road in an hour or so. Although he'd come to the Twin Cities once before since moving to Marquette, he did not stop by his home. He wound up staying too long with his friends and ran out of time to visit. He felt guilty about this and vowed to stop this time to ease his conscience.

As he pulled into the driveway, Jenkins saw his father, Ken, pulling a large red cooler from the back of a shiny silver Cadillac Escalade. He and his wife, Julie, had spent the day boating on Lake Minnetonka, a water playground for the well-to-do.

"Just get back from the lake?" asked John as he set his kickstand on the cement driveway.

"Sure did. What brings you here so soon? I wasn't expecting you for a few more hours."

"Oh, I'm a little tired and want to get back early. Did you catch the game?"

"Yeah, a solid win. I listened to the last inning on the radio on my way back from the lake. Give me a hand with this, and we'll go inside and have a drink."

Jenkins grabbed a bag of groceries while his father picked up the cooler and walked toward the garage. The far-left door of a four-stall garage was open, and the two walked through it. The inside of the garage was amazingly clean and housed only a few items, including two mountain bikes, some simple garden tools, and a long row of cabinets hanging over a workbench. His father set the cooler on the bench, which had on it only a toolbox, and it was closed.

"Let's go inside," he said, putting his hand lightly on his son's shoulder to guide him into the house. "Julie is shopping with the Ericksons, so she won't be home for a little while yet. I have some paperwork to finish up before Monday morning, so wanted to get a jump on it. What can I get you? Are you hungry?"

"No, I ate at the game. Just something to drink is fine," he said as he followed his father through a spacious kitchen filled with large stainless steel appliances, an Italian marble floor, a large center island with brass pots and pans hanging above it, and a large cherry dining set that matched the cabinetry.

"Beer, soda, tea? What'll it be?"

"Tea sounds good."

"Have a seat. I'll bring it out," he said as he pulled a large glass pitcher half filled with iced tea and floating lemons from the refrigerator.

John kicked off his shoes and walked through the dining area, which flowed into a glass-enclosed four-season porch. He sank into the puffy cushions of a costly wicker sofa, sprawled out his legs, and gazed onto the backyard, which resembled a nature sanctuary with its lush yet finely trimmed grass, a large flower garden in full bloom, and a hedgerow of pines and hardwoods that completely shielded the property from the neighbors. The elder Jenkins was proud of his landscaping and talked of it often, even though he did none of the work to maintain it, but rather hired it out.

"Here you go, John," said his father as he handed him a tall glass of iced tea with a napkin wrapped around it.

"Thanks." Jenkins took a sip, then put it down on a coaster on the end table.

"How's the job going?"

"It's fine."

"Don't worry. You'll be out of there soon. Just have to pay your dues."

"You should visit sometime."

"Yes, I know. But we've had a very busy month. Besides, there can't be too much to do there. Am I right?" said his father with a grin. While Ken wasn't overly disappointed with his son taking a job at the *Messenger*, he also wasn't overly supportive. He understood his reasoning but felt strongly that his son's skills and degree at least warranted a position with a daily newspaper in a larger city. "Maybe Julie and I can bring the boat down some long weekend, and you can meet us on the river."

"That'd be fun. When's the last time you've been out of the city?"

"Oh my, it's been awhile. Work keeps me pretty busy. Besides, everything I need is here."

John mulled around that thought and silently wondered if everything was here, indeed. All of his life his father promised to do things with him but rarely kept his word because his work schedule usually interfered with their plans. Although he knew the answer to the question he was about to ask, he asked it anyway.

"Have you ever thought about moving from the city? Maybe to a smaller town?"

"Never!" his father shot back. "I mean really, what opportunity exists in a small town? I think you've discovered that fairly quickly. Am I right?"

"I guess you are." Jenkins picked up his tea and took

94

another drink. Although he was ambitious and eager to make a name for himself, he always felt inferior to his father, who defined himself by his career. His father's life centered around his job, and he worked hard to climb to each higher rung of the ladder of success, often requiring sixty- to seventy-hour work-weeks. John thought of what that produced—a large house, expensive vehicles, luxurious vacations—but he questioned if it was worth the cost. The photo of Gutzman and his family flashed through his mind.

They lived meagerly, but they looked happy, he thought. *What about us? We have so much, but are we as happy?* He struggled to recall some memories of him and his father simply having fun together but could think of very few. All he could recall were outings with other families and large parties held in expensive homes and at country clubs.

"So you're happy with where you're at in life?"

"Happy? Of course I'm happy. I mean, look at what we've got. There aren't a lot of people who have what we have and who can afford to do the things we do, John. Look around you. I'd say we have a pretty good life." Then he paused as if the weight of his son's question finally sank in. "Why all this talk about happiness? Is everything okay, John?"

"Sure, everything is fine," he replied as the two heard the door to the garage open and close quietly. Julie walked into the kitchen, threw her keys on the counter, and strolled out to the porch. Her sun-bleached hair was perfectly combed back and bounced on her slender shoulders, and her toned legs flashed beneath her black sundress as she walked to a chair and sat down, crossing her right leg over the left. She was eleven years younger than his father and worked hard to keep up her appearance, even though the years of tanning and time in the sun were showing their effects on her skin, making it leathery brown.

"Hi, John. It's so great to see you," she said in a high,

bubbly voice. "Will you be staying tonight?"

"No, I've got to get goin' soon. I just stopped by for a few minutes to say hello. Did you have fun at the lake?"

"Oh yes. It was marvelous. You really must join us sometime. Maybe next weekend."

"I told John that we should take the boat down the river this summer and meet him in Marquette. How does that sound?"

"Oh, that sounds fun. But we'd need an extra day. Maybe the Bixbys would want to join us. Should I get my calendar?"

"Why don't we talk about it later? I think I'll be home next weekend," said Jenkins. "I've got some other commitments that I need to check on before we can set a date."

"That sounds fine, son. We'll find a weekend sometime this summer," said his father, as Julie flashed a big smile at him and nodded in agreement.

"Well, I better get going. I've got a long drive. I'll give you a call next weekend when I'm back and let you know when I'll be by."

"Okay, but we'll probably be at the lake most of the weekend again so make sure you try us on my cell phone," replied his father.

⌘⌘⌘

For the first half-hour of his drive back to Marquette, Jenkins mulled over the events of the day. He felt guilty for leaving his friends so quickly and tried to conjure up an excuse that would hold water the next time he saw them. He also thought about his childhood and of the time when his parents divorced. It was a bitter memory for him, one that still evoked much sadness and anger. He remembered the cold silence in the home before his mother moved out and then the vicious arguments his parents had over the following months as they fought through the terms of the divorce. His parents were both distant during that time and never shared a reason with him for their decision, other than to say that they weren't happy. Even though he was angry with his mother for leaving, he still missed her and promised himself that he would drive to Milwaukee in the coming months to visit her.

About halfway through his trip, his thoughts turned to Gutzman. As the miles raced by him and day faded into night, he felt angst over the simple obituary he had written. He spent the last twenty miles crafting a revised article in his mind and was eager to get to work the next day and put his thoughts on paper.

9

Jenkins pulled his bike into his usual spot in front of the *Messenger* office and sauntered up to the door, much the same way he did every other work day. He gave a hard tug on the handle, but the door didn't budge. On a second less aggressive pull, he heard the muffled clank of the metal lock as it caught against the frame. He glanced at his watch. *7:43.* Reaching into his pocket, he fished out his keys and found the brass one that fit the lock. He'd never before been the first one to arrive. The thought surprised him, and he shrugged.

The office was as quiet as he'd ever heard it. All that was audible was the gentle hum of the computer server and the soft drone of one of the overhead fluorescent lights as it slowly flickered, trying to draw enough energy to become fully lit. He walked slowly to his desk, then turned abruptly toward the coffee machine, where he pulled the pot away from it and filled it in the nearby bathroom sink. Upon his return, he poured the bubbly water, now milky looking, into the receptacle, scooped two heaps of grounds into the filter, and flipped the switch. Just then he heard the front door open.

Berg appeared, looking puzzled. "John, that is you," he said, as if answering his own question. "I thought that was your motorcycle. You're here early."

"Yeah, I guess I am. Good morning, Steve."

"Did you have a nice weekend?" asked Berg, unusually chatty. Berg was a personable and friendly man, but Jenkins knew he typically didn't engage in small talk, especially with his employees. He was normally the first one in the office each day and was busy working by the time the others arrived. They would pass by his office and offer their morning greetings, but he merely returned the sentiment and rarely said much more.

"Yeah, I did," answered Jenkins.

"How'd the parade shoot go? I didn't see you there."

"It was fine. I got all the shots you asked for."

"Great. I hope it didn't cut into your plans too much. You went to the Twins games, right?"

"Well, I made one of the two. Got tied up on Saturday. Sunday's game was great, though. Did you watch it?"

"Heard it on the radio. It looks like they might have a good year if the pitching holds up."

The familiar squeak of the door announced the arrival of Rachel and Frank, who came in discussing one of Frank's newest advertising clients, a small children's clothing store that recently opened in the former space of Ray's Shoe Repair, located on Second Street, two blocks down. As they rounded the corner from the reception area they both paused and gave Jenkins the same astonished look that Berg had greeted him with moments earlier. Frank glanced quickly at his watch, while Rachel shot a look toward the clock on the wall.

"Are the clocks right?" Rachel said, directing the comment toward their boss.

"Yep. John's the early bird this morning. Even made coffee."

"Well, I'll be," she said, looking at Jenkins and grinning. "I guess you *can* get up early."

The foursome smiled.

"John, I didn't think you had it in you," Frank said, slapping him on the back on his way to his desk.

The phone rang, and Rachel scurried to answer it while the others turned toward their day's work.

Jenkins' normal Monday morning routine involved calling for the city council agenda or that of the school board or county board of commissioners, depending on the week, and rewriting some news releases, but he abandoned that schedule so he could work on the article he had rewritten in his mind the night before. He opened the file on Gutzman and reread its contents:

Gutzman Found Dead in Oakhaven Cemetery

Alfred Gutzman was found dead Friday morning in the Oakhaven Cemetery, 1854 Pine Street. Wabasha County Sheriff Don Pittman discovered his body at approximately 6 a.m. near the grave of his wife and son. Wabasha County Medical Examiner Rick Clark said Gutzman died of a severe heart attack. He was 88.

According to Mike Fallwell, funeral director with Breckman and Fallwell Funeral Home, Gutzman emigrated from Hamburg, Germany, to Marquette in 1945, following WWII, and purchased a farmstead on the north end of town near the city limits. He married Mildred Knutson of Marquette and they had one child, Frederick, who was killed during the Vietnam War in 1967. Mildred died when the tornado of 1985 hit their homestead, destroying much of it, as well as a good portion of the northern end of Marquette. Gutzman has no living relatives.

Pathetic, he said to himself. *It doesn't even say anything about the man.*

By this time the office was abuzz with activity. He could hear Rachel on her second phone call of the morning, Berg clicking away on his computer, and Frank espousing the marketing benefits of the *Messenger* to another prospective client. Frank, a middle-aged man with thinning hair, was always well dressed and had a strong, confident personality and a boisterous way of selling himself and the paper. There was only a single partition between his and Jenkins' desk, so Jenkins could always hear Frank's entire conversations, and oftentimes even the voice on the other end of the line if he listened hard enough.

At first it had been very distracting to Jenkins as he tried to concentrate on his writing, but by now he was used to it. He tuned out Frank's chatter and began to construct his story. After entering some information and massaging the text, he stopped working, remembering he hadn't yet checked his voice mail. He dialed the number and discovered there was only one message on it, left at 8:10 a.m. on Saturday.

"Hello, this is Nancy Potter from the library," it said. "I found out this morning that Alfred Gutzman passed away yesterday. I thought you might like to know. He was a generous supporter of the library and our programs. I believe the funeral will be on Monday at St. Paul's Lutheran. You can call Cathy Crosby at the church office for more details. And, oh yes, please change the time of our summer reading program to Wednesday afternoons at three. You had the time wrong in last week's paper. Thank you."

"I don't believe it. Everyone knew this guy," said Jenkins as he rifled through a file of last week's news releases. "Ah ha! Here it is. Summer reading program every Wednesday at *two p.m.*, just what I thought."

Rachel returned with the mail and flashed her eyes at Jenkins as she walked into Berg's office and laid the rubber-banded bundle on his desk. The door was open, as it always was, and he could hear them talking.

"Steve, would it be okay if I took off a few hours this morning? I'd like to attend Mr. Gutzman's funeral at my church."

"Absolutely, Rachel. That will be fine. What time is it?"

"It's at ten o'clock, but I'd like to stay afterward and help with the luncheon."

"That's fine. Take as much time as you need."

Rachel rarely asked for time off, so Berg was always quick to grant her requests when she had one.

Why would she go? Jenkins asked himself as he pushed back his chair and followed her to the reception desk. "Did I hear you say you're going to Gutzman's funeral?"

"You heard right. Those are some good ears you have."

"But why? I didn't know that you knew him *that* well."

"You never asked," she said sharply. ""He was from my church. I've known him practically all my life, and I want to pay my respects."

Again, the phone clattered, and Rachel grabbed it before its second ring. Jenkins walked back to his desk and sat down, thinking about the funeral service, now less than an hour away.

Should I go? Terrell invited me. But why would I? Jenkins wrestled with his thoughts. He wanted to go because he had learned so much about this man over the past few days, yet thought he would feel out of place, a stranger. Then he reasoned that the experience would help him with his article, so he approached Berg with the same request as Rachel's.

"What? Why do *you* want to go?" asked Berg, shocked at the request. "You didn't even know him. Besides, if I recall, you weren't even too thrilled with writing a short obituary about him."

"I know. It sounds strange, but I've learned a lot about him over the weekend. I wrote the obit on Friday but came in early this morning to rewrite it because I think there's a bigger story to be told about this man. I think I need to go to the funeral so I can put the finishing touches on it."

"Have you started your parade piece yet?"

"Not yet, but that won't take long. I'll just stay for the funeral and come back right after. I'll even work through my lunch hour if you want me to."

"I guess that's fine. So what have you learned about him

that's so interesting?"

"You'll find out when you read the story," said Jenkins, smiling, as he left Berg's office and turned back to his article.

About two sentences into his story, Rachel patched through a call to him.

"John, there's a Mr. Johanson on the line for you."

"Thanks," he said, while pushing the blinking line on hold. "John Jenkins," he answered confidently.

"John, this is Darrel Johanson. You're the one who writes about the city council meetings, right?"

"That's right. How can I help you?"

"Well, I think you should write a story about the assessment they're doing on my block. We're at the edge of town on Kellogg Street, right on the city limit border. We don't need sidewalks on our block. It's ridiculous."

"I remember the council discussing that at the last meeting but don't recall anyone there in opposition."

"We just learned about it."

"Who's we?"

"My neighbors and I. There are five of us on this block, and we all think it's a crazy idea. I think those boys are just looking for some extra cash for their pet projects."

"Are you planning to attend the next meeting?"

"You bet."

"How many of you?"

"Well, we're all going to try to make it."

"That's great. It sounds like something we'd consider. I'll talk to my editor and get back to you. What's your phone number?"

"465-1966. Are you going to write about this?"

"Like I said, I think I probably will, but I need to talk with my editor and get more details."

"Well, I hope you do. This is an important issue. I hope to hear from you soon."

"I'm sure you will. I'd also like to talk to some of your neighbors. Do you think you can get me their names?"

"Sure. Of course."

"Your name is Darrel Johanson, right?"

"That's right."

"Is it J-0-H-A-N-S-O-N?"

"That's correct."

"Great. Thanks for the call. I've got to go to a meeting now. I'll be in touch."

He looked at the clock, which read 9:44, and jumped up and scampered out the door. Rachel had left a minute or two earlier and he could see her walking a block away, turning right onto Fourth Street, which led directly to the church, only six blocks away from the *Messenger* office.

Jenkins ran to catch up with her. "Hey, wait up," he called as he approached her.

"What's up?"

"I'm going with you, if that's okay."

"What?"

"I thought I'd go to the funeral. Do you think that's okay?"

"Ah sure. I guess so. But why do *you* want to go?"

"I don't know really. It's just that since I first heard about Gutzman's death on Friday, it seems everywhere I've gone lately I've run into someone who has something to say about him. I wrote an obituary about him on Friday, but it's small, incomplete. I think he deserves more, and I think this will help me understand who he was. Sounds strange, huh?"

"Maybe a little, but I understand."

"So, how *do* you know him?"

"Mostly through church. He was my Sunday school teacher when I was in sixth grade. He was a really neat man. Soft-spoken, very nice, and easy to talk to. He always had a twinkle in his eye whenever I saw him; that I will always remember. And he loved to whistle. I don't think he ever did it much around people, but I would often catch him doing it in his classroom before we came in for Sunday school, when he thought others weren't around. He was a really good whistler."

"Rach, I can't believe it. It seems like everyone knew this guy. I'm beginning to wish I could have met him."

"It's too bad you didn't have the chance. He was a special man."

"What else?"

"Oh, I don't know. He was one of those neat old guys that was always around, always helping out. I remember he'd stand on the steps outside the church talking and laughing with the other older men, but he was always the first to lend a hand when something needed to be done, like setting up more tables and chairs or helping the ladies take leftover food to their cars."

"I see," Jenkins said, trying to envision the scene as they walked side-by-side down the sidewalk, past small ramblers and story-and-a-half homes half hidden by large, bushy trees.

The church was less than a block away now. Jenkins squinted in the sharp morning sunlight at the sign and remembered his near accident two days earlier and faintly smiled at the thought of it. They walked in silence the remaining distance, as seemed appropriate, considering where they were going. The warm sunshine washed over them, and birds chirped noisily in the trees above. To Jenkins, the bright, clear day seemed out-of-place for what he thought a funeral day should be like. *This is strange,* he thought as they crossed the street to the church. *Instead of sun and noisy birds, the day should hold dark, heavy clouds and rain and thunder.* It was the first funeral Jenkins had ever attended.

There was only one other couple—an elderly, white-haired man and his graying wife—approaching the church at the same time as Jenkins and Rachel. The man was the first one to reach the door, so he held it open for his wife and then motioned for Jenkins and Rachel to go through. Inside, a wide flight of stairs led to the narthex. Alongside the narthex was a large coatroom, now empty except for one scarf on a hanger and a man's hat on a wire shelf. To the side of the cloakroom was a restroom for each of the sexes. Near a pair of open doors that led to the sanctuary was Gutzman's casket, with the lid open.

Jenkins was shocked to see the open casket. From where he was standing, he could just make out the form of the body. He stood silently at a safe distance, alternating awkward glances to and away from the body. He watched as the couple that entered the church before them casually approached the casket and stood over it while reverently looking at the body inside. The wife clutched her husband's arm at the elbow and settled in slightly behind him as they gazed in, evidently recalling some lasting memory of the man inside.

Rachel touched his arm. The expression in her eyes was sympathetic. She could sense that he was uncomfortable. "I'm going to go over. Do you want to go or wait here?"

He stammered slightly while debating the idea in his mind. "Sure, I'll go."

Rachel led the way. She walked slowly to the casket, her eyes fixed on Gutzman the entire time, and stopped about one foot away. She folded her hands loosely at her waist as she looked in.

Jenkins stood about two feet behind Rachel but was still close enough to get an entire view of the body. The casket had a rich, shiny mahogany finish and a plush, off-white interior that was ruffled and appeared to be heavily padded.

Jenkins' eyes were first drawn to Gutzman's hands, which were interlocked near his beltline. His fingers looked hard and bony and his nails glossy, looking almost as if they'd been polished. He slowly moved his gaze up and examined the blue suit he was wearing. He remembered looking in his closet and wondered if this was one of the suits he'd seen hanging there.

Finally, he summoned the courage to look at Gutzman's

face. It looked much different than what he'd seen in the portrait at his house. His gray hair was combed tightly back over the top of his head and around his ears, which looked big. The color of his skin was pale and jaundiced and did not completely absorb the makeup that the mortician used to mask his lifelessness. His eyelids were closed unusually tight and his lips were pursed and thin.

It was hard for Jenkins to imagine the light and laughter that once danced inside the man, something that so many people remembered about him. The absolute stillness of Gutzman's body was disturbing. Jenkins had to look away, so he turned to Rachel.

"Should we go in?" he said, taking a half step toward the sanctuary.

"Yes. Let's go in now," she said, wiping a tear from her eye.

10

Walking through a pair of heavy, dark wooden doors into the sanctuary, Jenkins was surprised to see that the church was completely filled with people. Most of them were elderly, but there were several middle-aged couples and even a few families with young children. They all sat quietly, eyes forward, waiting for the service to begin.

"Who are all these people? I didn't think he had any family," he whispered as he leaned toward Rachel.

She turned her head toward him and murmured, "People from the community. Many are from our church."

An usher who was dressed in a wrinkled black suit approached them, handed them a bulletin, and pointed to an area near the middle of the church where they could sit together. They quickly took their seats as melancholy notes droned from an organ and echoed throughout the church, forming a tune unfamiliar to Jenkins. The funeral director and the ushers wheeled Gutzman's closed casket to the front of the church. As Jenkins scanned the crowd, he began to feel increasingly uncomfortable and wished he hadn't come. It had been several years since he'd been to a church service, and he felt out of place.

As the musical prelude subsided, Pastor Terrell entered from a side door behind the pulpit and approached the casket. On it was a white linen cloth folded in thirds. The pastor stood by as the funeral director slowly unfolded the cloth and ironed it with his hands until the cloth completely covered the casket. Terrell was dressed in an off-white robe gathered around his waist with a braided rope tied at his side and looped over itself. His robe flowed behind him as he walked from the casket to the center of the altar. At first Jenkins didn't recognize him. He looked much different than the day he met him standing in the warm summer sun in front of the church, with beads of perspiration rolling off his brow. Now he looked dignified and walked with an air of gentle authority.

"Welcome to the house of the Lord. This is a day that the Lord hath made. Let us be joyful and be glad in it."

Joyful? thought Jenkins. *What an odd thing to say.*

"We are here today to celebrate the life of Alfred Gutzman—the life he had with us while here on earth, but more importantly the life he is now living with Jesus Christ, our Lord and Savior. Please join me in singing hymn number 593, 'Why Do We Mourn Departed Friends.'"

By the time the organ started bellowing the tune, nearly everyone in the congregation had turned to the page and was ready to sing. Jenkins, however, fumbled with the hymnal, flipping through its pages to find the hymn. He finally found the page as the rest of the people assembled joined their voices in unison:

"Why do we mourn departed friends
Or shake at death's alarms?
"'Tis but the voice that Jesus sends
To call them to His arms.

Are we not tending upward, too,
As fast as time can move?
Nor would we wish the hours more slow
To keep us from our Love.

Why should we tremble to convey
Their bodies to the tomb?

There the dear flesh of Jesus lay
And scattered all the gloom.

The graves of all the saints He blest
And softened every bed.
Where should the dying members rest
But with their dying Head?

Thence he arose, ascending high,
And showed our feet the way.
Up to the Lord we, too, shall fly
At the great rising-day.

Then let the last loud trumpet sound
And bid our kindred rise:
Awake ye nations under ground!
Ye saints, ascend the skies!"

Much of the service followed a written order that was interspersed between the hymnal and a freshly printed bulletin. Jenkins attempted to follow along but became frustrated and finally gave up. Rachel tried to help him by motioning to either the hymnal or the bulletin at the appropriate time. He was relieved when the other members returned their hymnbooks to the wooden racks on the pew backs, and Pastor Terrell entered the pulpit. As he stepped into the elevated platform, he paused with his head bowed, as if in prayer, then looked out on the congregation and began to speak:

"'Why do we mourn departing friends or shake at death's alarms? 'Tis but the voice that Jesus sends to call them to His arms.' Those are sweet and poignant lyrics of a beautiful hymn—lyrics that follow our tradition here at St. Paul's, as we prepare to commit a loved one to eternal rest. And while this is a time of mourning because we miss our dear friend and understand that we will no longer share precious moments with him, it really is a time to rejoice because the soul of a fellow believer has crossed the threshold to eternal life and now rests in peace with our Lord and Savior, Jesus Christ. Blessed is the name of the Lord and praise be to God, our maker and redeemer.

"I'll never forget the day I first had the opportunity to minister to Alfred. I had only been in town for a few weeks when the tornado of '85 hit his farm, taking his wife and destroying much of his property. I know many of you remember that day because you and your families were affected as well. It was a difficult time for our community and an extremely difficult time for Alfred.

"I remember sitting on his back steps, trying in vain to find words of comfort to share with him, but everything I said seemed totally inadequate. And in the end, I believe the words he said to me offered the greatest amount of hope and assurance to both of us. Through red and tearful eyes he looked at me, smiled, and said, 'Well, she made it.'

"It was a simple phrase; anything but eloquent. But I knew what he meant and could think of no better words to express the bittersweet joy of the moment. You see, he knew that his blessed bride had lived a life of faith. And because of that faith, she was taken to heaven.

"Scripture is clear on this point. In Romans, chapter 10, the Apostle Paul assures us that 'if you confess with your mouth, 'Jesus is Lord' and believe in your heart that God raised Him from the dead, you will be saved. For it is with your heart that you believe and are justified, and it is with your mouth that you confess and are saved.' And in Ephesians, Paul also says: 'By grace you have been saved through faith; and this is not from yourselves, it is the gift of God.'

"I had many conversations with Alfred since that day and I know that he, too, had that unshakable faith. He lived his life with an eye toward heaven, and now I'm confident that he is in paradise with our Lord and Savior."

Jenkins hadn't given much thought to the notion of an afterlife, but these words penetrated deep into his soul and confused him. From what he knew about religion, it was based on moral laws and high ideals that nobody could possibly attain, thus leaving people filled with guilt and shame for not living up to its expectations. It was because of this, he had told himself many years ago, that he wanted no part of it. Yet he wondered why faith had played such an important role in Gutzman's life.

Could that *have been their faith?* he questioned, remembering the unexplainable expression he saw in the faces of the Gutzman family portrait. *There* was *something different about them.*

The rest of Pastor Terrell's sermon was focused on what he called the "comfort from the cross," the sermon theme printed in the bulletin. Jenkins was surprised that he did not reflect more on Gutzman's life, yet was compelled by what he heard and found consolation in the message.

At the end of the service, the funeral director walked to the casket and slowly refolded the funeral pall, much the same way as he unfolded it; in thirds and ironing each fold with his hands. When finished, he stepped aside and two pallbearers somberly approached the casket and wheeled it back to the narthex while the congregation sang "How Great Thou Art," a tune Jenkins had recognized from somewhere in his past, likely from an old television program. According to Pastor Terrell, it was Gutzman's favorite hymn, and it was evident that the congregation loved it, too, because they sang louder and louder with each stanza.

Then, as the final stanza approached, Pastor Terrell motioned for the people to rise. Standing straight and tall, they passionately belted out the last refrain. To Jenkins, it seemed as if it were only one thunderous voice singing the song, filling the sanctuary with electricity and emotion. The pastor faced the congregation, visibly moved by the chorus of praise, and stood silently to let the full wonder of the moment fill the people.

"Beautiful. How great Thou art indeed," he said with a crackle in his voice, now facing the congregation. He raised both hands above his head and continued. "May the Lord bless you and keep you. May He make his face shine upon you and be gracious to you. May the Lord look upon you with favor and give you His peace. Amen.

"The congregation is invited to the committal ceremony at the Oakhaven Cemetery immediately following the service, and then a light luncheon in the church basement provided by the Ladies' Aid."

"Are you going to the cemetery?" Jenkins whispered to Rachel, as the ushers were dismissing people, row by row, starting from the front of the sanctuary.

"No, I need to help prepare the lunch. I told my mom I'd help. Are you going to stay?"

"Oh, I don't know. I told Steve I wouldn't be gone that long."

"Okay, but it is almost lunchtime," she said, as if trying to convince him to stay.

"Are most of these people going to the cemetery?"

"Oh, I doubt it. Many will stay here. We'll have coffee while we wait, so you can stay for a cup even if you don't want one of our famous ham salad sandwiches."

"Maybe I will come down for just one cup."

⌘ ⌘ ⌘

The fellowship hall was a long, deep open space with a beige tile floor and only a few half-windows that let the sunlight in. The only things that gave the room depth were the steel support posts placed every twelve feet apart across the width and breadth of the room. The hall was lined with long wooden tables covered with paper tablecloths that draped over the sides and touched the seats of the metal folding chairs placed around them. No attempt was made to arrange the tables to accommodate traffic flow or conversation; they were simply lined up end on end to allow for full capacity.

On the far end of the room was the kitchen, now teeming with activity. Gray-haired women danced and wove around each other as if their movements were choreographed. As one pulled a pan of sandwiches from the refrigerator, another was there to snatch it from her and run it to one of two serving tables. Others stood in a traffic-free zone, poured coffee and milk, and cut brownies and marbled cake into three-inch squares. Once on a plate, another woman was there to whisk it away.

The ladies had determined, almost competitive, expressions as they went about their duties—and it was evident they were in their element by their speed and efficiency. From the time it had taken to sing the verses of the final hymn of the service, this finely tuned assembly line had the food laid out and ready to serve. A dozen coffee pots were filled and waiting as the first of the attendees came down and milled around, engaging in conversation. Others took a seat and talked to each other from across the table. The women made sure that everyone who wanted coffee was attended to and refreshed often.

As soon as Jenkins and Rachel got to the fellowship hall, the room was filled with chatter. While he knew that Rachel had duties to attend to in the kitchen, he was caught by surprise at how quickly she left him. He felt awkward in the midst of the strangers around him and quickly decided to leave. Then a hand touched him on his shoulder.

"I thought that was you," said Sandy, the waitress from the café. She was wearing a long, black dress that complimented her figure, and she looked much prettier than the times he'd seen her before. She was with her son, who was standing slightly behind her, yet his head towered above hers. "John, I'd like you to meet my son, Josh."

"Nice to meet you, Josh," he said as they shook hands.

"Same here," the young man replied, not making eye contact.

"John, I'm a bit surprised to see you here. Would you like to sit with us?"

"Sure. I can't stay long, but I would like a cup of coffee."

"Sit down, all of you, I'll get it for you," said one of the gray-haired servers who had evidently eavesdropped on the conversation. "Would you like some also, Sandy?"

"Yes, Marge. That'd be wonderful. Thanks."

"And you, young man? Would you like juice or milk?"

"No thanks."

The three of them sat down and began to make small talk when another hand tapped Jenkins on his shoulder.

"Hi, John. It's nice to see you," said Roberta Hendrickson, the city clerk. Although he had only met her in person a few times, Jenkins spoke with Roberta weekly, if not more. She was a valuable asset to him as he tracked down leads and sources for his weekly coverage of the city government.

"Roberta, hi. How are you?" he asked. "Would you like to join us?"

"No, I'm on my way over to my Ladies' Aid friends over there," she replied, motioning toward a group of six older women gossiping with each other two tables away. She smiled at Sandy and nodded as if to excuse herself for the interruption. "I just wanted to say hello."

"I'm glad you did. Thanks. I'll talk to you soon."

"Yes, we'll talk soon, John. Nice to see you, Sandy," she

said, placing her hand lightly on Sandy's shoulder before she headed for her friends.

Before he and Sandy could resume their conversation, Jerry Peterson approached them, coffee in hand, along with Pastor Terrell and Fred Mallard, whom Terrell introduced as one of the church elders. Jenkins didn't exactly know what that meant but assumed it was a church leadership position, since he was one of few people there who wore a plastic badge with his name and title printed on it.

The group sat down and began reminiscing about Gutzman's life. With permission, Jenkins ripped off a section of the paper tablecloth and began to scribble notes. When others standing nearby heard the conversation, they would come over, sit down, and share their memories as well. Jenkins would ask a simple question, like: "What did he do in his free time?" and it was as if he had opened a floodgate. Recollections flowed like water from a broken spout and Jenkins couldn't write fast enough to record them all.

The minutes had turned into an hour and Jenkins had torn off the entire section of tablecloth surrounding him when his cell phone rang. Surprised, he quickly pulled it from his pocket.

"Hello?"

"John. Where the heck are you? We've got a deadline to meet, you know," said Berg in an angry, thunderous tone.

Jenkins winced. It wasn't the first time Berg had to reel him in around deadline time, so he could get his stories edited and prepared for pagination of the paper before sending it to the printer.

"Steve, hi. I'm still at the funeral," he said, while standing up and walking away so the rest of the people at the table wouldn't hear his scolding.

"What? You said you'd be back in one hour, and it's already been over two. What's going on?"

"Sorry, time got away from me. I've been talking to people

116

about Gutzman, for my story."

"Oh boy. I hope you're about finished, because I really need you back here. I need those stories."

"Yes, absolutely. I'm on my way."

He closed his phone, returned it to his pocket, and approached the table, gathering up his disheveled notes.

"Deadline calls. Gotta go. It was a pleasure meeting all of you. You've been a big help for my story. I feel like I know Mr. Gutzman a little better now after talking with all of you," he said and swiftly headed for the door.

Those at the table in the fellowship hall watched Jenkins walk away.

"He seems like a pretty good kid," said one of the older men, a farmer whose white biceps peeked through his short-sleeve shirt as he extended his arms on the table.

The others nodded in agreement.

11

Jenkins walked briskly back to his office, retracing the same route that he and Rachel had taken to the church. He knew Berg was going to be irate with him for being late, but he also knew that the notes and experience he had at the funeral would make his story immensely better than what it would have been, had he not attended. He'd learned much about Gutzman and the contributions he'd made to the community from his recent conversations and was eager to add this new information to his story. However, there was still one piece of the puzzle missing that nagged at him, but he was quite sure he knew where he could find the answer to the question: from the journal he'd discovered at the Gutzman farm.

As he approached the office, he could see Berg through a window, pacing from his office to the production area, as he customarily did several times every Monday afternoon at deadline. He'd finish editing a story, save the file, and then go to the production computer where Margaret, the paper's production manager, was busy typesetting ads and placing stories into her layout template on the computer. Berg would let her know which file could be placed next, what page he wanted it on, and watch to see if his headline fit the space, which it almost always did perfectly.

Jenkins fished around in his pocket, pulled out his key, and jumped on his bike. As the engine roared, he could see Berg peer out the window to see him pulling away from the office.

He was sure he could hear Berg's blood boiling.

Jenkins boldly drove into the Gutzman farmstead, this time with little regard for being seen. It was broad daylight, and he knew an inconspicuous approach was impossible. Parking his bike behind the barn, out of sight from the highway, he hurried to the house and strode through the kitchen and living room without paying much attention to anything except the family portrait on the wall.

He leaped up the steps and plopped down on his knees in front of the cedar chest that he had rested against while reading the journal on his first intrusion into the home. He grasped both sides of the lid and slowly opened it, seeing what he somehow knew would be there: a stack of journals, mixed in among a variety of other items, including two photo albums, various articles of clothing, and some children's toys. There were two stacks, both containing six or seven journals each. He grabbed the pile on the right and examined the covers—some red, some blue, and some green. All were dated. He gently put them back in place, making them look as if he'd never handled them, then lifted the other pile from the chest. He found the one with the oldest date and opened its cover. It read:

> My wife and son are with the Lord. I have no family to pass on my name or fortune to, yet I feel compelled to write down the details of my life.

Jenkins scanned the first few pages of entries, which listed simple biographical information: birthdate, place of birth, the names of his parents and three siblings. Entries near the middle of the journal included notes on his schooling, childhood memories, confirmation date, and even his first kiss. Jenkins furiously scribbled notes while perusing the pages, then thumbed to the end of the notebook where he found the memoirs of Gutzman's military experience. He stopped speed-reading and slowly pored over the entries, completely digesting their contents. Much of it was drab and rather dry: enlistment date, rank, training, etc., but then he came to the last entry, one of few that was titled.

The Decision of My Life

Thinking back now, it's hard to imagine the power one man, Hitler, had over a country. But one must remember that my country, Germany, was in dire economic turmoil at the time. Over one-third of our workforce was unemployed. So many felt hopeless, and he preached a message of hope. He told us that we were a strong nation, that we were a great nation, and that he would get us working again, which he did. So many of us believed in our country and wanted to work, and we were willing to fight to make it strong. That's why I enlisted.

However, it wasn't long before people, like my parents, began to see through his facade. I remember listening to him on the radio and hearing my father repeat time after time, "This man is evil; he does not have the will of God in mind." There were several others in our church and community with the same sentiment, but most were less vocal and remained relatively quiet, living in fear of being branded a traitor.

As a young man, I didn't look closely enough at Hitler's political views but only at the good he was doing for our nation. I supported him because I saw him building a stronger country. But I'll never forget the day I saw the true face of evil.

I was on a troop transport train that stopped in Dachau to lend aid to the soldiers stationed there. We had heard the rumors of the Jews being taken to this camp, but I was surprised to see the large number of them when we arrived. Their faces showed fear, a terrible fear, as our soldiers separated them from each other: women in one direction, young children in another, and the men in another, being pushed around like a herd of animals. I can still see those young children clinging tightly to their mother's skirts, screaming, crying ferociously, not wanting to leave. The soldiers were barking orders to them, saying they must separate for safety and to be fed. Then they pried the children from the arms of their wailing mothers.

It was overcast and rainy, and the entire compound was nothing but mud. As we left the train, we walked through the hysteria, and the stench of those people soaked in sweat, urine, and feces made me gag.

Three other soldiers and I were sent to keep order in the showering area after we ate. First we found the kitchen and had a large, hot meal of wiener schnitzel and sauerkraut, then we reported to our duty area.

It was a humiliating sight to see those poor souls when we arrived—a long line of gaunt, naked men, heads shaven, cowering in line with their hands over their private areas. Two of us were stationed near the front of the line, two near the end. I was at the front, by the door, and it was my job to usher them through and then lock the door behind them once they were all inside, which I did, not thinking much about it.

I remember feeling confused about what was happening when I heard the muffled sounds of weeping and moaning from within and the constant pounding on the thick, steel door. But I didn't know or understand what was taking place.

Several minutes later, a husky young lieutenant with steely blue eyes charged in, followed by a dozen other soldiers. He ordered me to open the door. When I did, I could feel a heaviness against it. I opened it, and several bodies tumbled toward me. I was horrified by what I saw. Inside, all those men were dead, and many were heaped on top of each other by the door. One of them twitched, as if he still had a strain of life in him, and the startled lieutenant pulled his pistol from his belt and shot him in the head.

I remember screaming at him, "What is this?"

It was the first and only time I ever questioned an officer. For my remark, he hit me on the side of my head with his pistol and knocked me to the ground. He spat on me and told me to get the "stinking carcasses" out of there and bury them in the trench behind the building. Then he stormed out at fast as he came in.

The memories of pulling those men from that room and putting them into a mass grave are very painful to remember, and it still makes me nauseous even to recall it. As I helped throw the bodies into the pit, I prayed for forgiveness for myself, my country, and for the souls of those men. I began to vomit so severely that I was pulled from the line and ridiculed by many of the other soldiers.

I vowed that day would be my last as a German soldier.

Jenkins put down the journal and looked inward to envision the horrific scene....

⌘ ⌘ ⌘

Gutzman wiped the vomit from his chin with the back of his wool-mitted hand as a tear slid down his wind-burned cheek. His right hand was still gripping a shovel tightly, a tool that had supported his weight as he heaved from disgust over what he had just seen, and what he had just done. He could hear the other soldiers in his detail laughing at him and cursing him intermittently. One hacked up a mouthful of mucus and saliva and spat it on his back as he walked by him, angry that he had to do extra work due to Gutzman's absence. They called him a woman and a coward, but the remarks meant nothing to him now.

He straightened himself completely and stared up at the muddy brown sky. *Oh, God. Forgive me. What have I done?*

From the corner of his eye he could see the other soldiers throwing more bodies into the wide earthen pit. They tossed them in as if they were throwing bags of flour or potatoes onto a truck bed, showing no regard for the dead. Gutzman couldn't bring himself to look at the scene, so he turned away, his stomach again knotting in pain. He choked and gagged, his mouth watering profusely, but his stomach had already emptied itself completely so he could vomit no more. He closed his eyes tightly and crow's feet formed around his eyes above his youthful cheeks.

Oh, God. What have I done? Forgive me, he prayed again.

Gutzman had been in several fierce battles during his short military career and had seen many close friends lose an arm or a leg, or their life, from a bullet, grenade, or bomb blast. He himself had been shot in the upper right thigh and had killed men at point-blank range, men who were close enough that he could see the fear in their eyes. The killing bothered him but not to the point of mental anguish because he understood it to

123

be a necessary part of war. However, the shameful killing that he'd just experienced was much different. These people were civilians: harmless, naked, and unable to defend themselves. The image of the dead men spilling out from against the shower door flashed through his mind, and the muffled screams of the room invaded his thoughts.

Dear God, I can't be part of this any longer. I must leave.

It was at that moment that Gutzman began to construct a plan to defect, a thought that had never before entered his mind. He threw down his shovel and walked away.

⌘⌘⌘

From the pages of the journal, Gutzman went on to tell about the scheme he devised to leave the camp, the help he received from a fellow soldier that allowed him to sneak out of the camp in the dark of night, the hazardous path he followed to the Swiss border, and the obstacles he had to overcome along the way, including hiding in a flooded ditch from a German convoy, being attacked from a protective farmyard dog while stealing eggs, which he ate raw for nourishment, and his final push across the border, where he was fired upon by German guards.

Suddenly, Jenkins heard a sound from downstairs. It sounded like the click of a closing door, followed by muffled footsteps shuffling across the floor. He returned the journals to the chest, closed the lid silently, and crouched down by the steps, making sure he was out of sight from anyone looking upstairs. He thought about stealing away to Gutzman's room and hiding behind some of the clothes in the closet but quickly decided against it. Whoever was downstairs was making his way boldly through the house, undoubtedly looking for the owner of the motorcycle parked outside. He could hear the footsteps approach the staircase, so he peeked his head around the corner and looked downstairs.

"Who's there?" a booming voice beckoned, followed by the rushing of feet as the man ducked beyond the stairwell, as if seeking protection.

"My name is John Jenkins. Who are you?"

"This is Sergeant Williams with the Marquette Police Department," he screamed back. "Show yourself!"

Jenkins walked slowly to the stairs and could see Williams at the bottom, with his gun held tightly in his right fist, supported firmly on top of his left palm. His finger was on the trigger, and he was pointing the weapon directly at Jenkins.

The sight shocked Jenkins, and he instinctively raised his hands and muttered, "Whoa! I'm not armed."

"Walk slowly down the steps and keep your hands where I can see them," demanded Williams.

Jenkins did as he was told and came face-to-face with Williams at the bottom of the stairs.

Evidently Williams realized he wasn't in danger, for he lowered his weapon, and his guard. "May I ask what you're doing here," he said, with a hint of arrogance.

"It's kind of a long story," replied Jenkins, hoping he wouldn't have to repeat it all. Since the time he'd been in the house, Berg had tried to reach him four times on his cell phone. He let each call go to his voicemail, knowing his boss was going to be even more angry with him for doing that.

"Well, luckily for you I have a lot of time. Do you realize you're trespassing on private property?"

"Yes, and I'm sorry. Like I said, I'm John Jenkins. I'm a reporter for the *Messenger*, and I'm here doing research on Mr. Gutzman."

"Show me some ID," Williams said gruffly.

Jenkins pulled out his wallet, removed his license and his press card, and handed them both to Williams.

"I recognize the name. You just started doing the police reports, right?"

"Yeah, I pick 'em up and compile 'em."

It was one of Jenkins' weekly duties to visit the police department, which was connected to city hall, to get the police reports. It was the paper's policy to publish each report as provided, including the names of the offenders. This policy made the page popular with the subscribers but more than once got the paper into hot water when one of the town's prominent residents appeared for a DWI, writing a bad check, or some other misdemeanor crime that likely caused more controversy than harm in the community. "Anyway, I'm writing an obituary on Mr. Gutzman, and I was here snooping around to get more information about him. As you probably already know, he doesn't have any relatives."

Willams was a ten-year veteran with the department. In his late thirties and extremely fit, he sported a tight crew cut, similar to the one he wore in the Marine Corps while serving overseas during the first Persian Gulf War. His uniform was crisp and sharp and reminiscent of his military days. His military training had a profound impact on him, and he wore his position of authority on his sleeve like a badge of honor.

"That's right. He doesn't," Williams said as he holstered his weapon, which he was now holding loosely at his side. He took a deep breath, relieved that the situation was harmless.

"He was a good man," Williams said. "Honest and caring. Did you know he would visit prisoners in the jail at least once a month?"

"No, I didn't know that."

"Yeah, he would bring them books and magazines and Bibles from his church, I think. He'd spend at least an hour talking to them. He didn't care who they were or what they'd done. He had a heck of a lot more compassion for them than I do."

Jenkins checked his watch. "Listen, I'm sorry I intruded, but the door *was* unlocked. I'm on deadline. Do you mind if I go? My boss is gonna kill me for being late."

The appeal irked Williams. His immediate reaction was to detain Jenkins even longer to teach him a lesson about the consequences of questioning authority. He was ready to give Jenkins a piece of his mind, but quickly thought of what his chief would say if he brought the young reporter into the station. He knew the chief would be more lenient in this situation.

Williams relaxed. "Yeah, I guess you can go. It's not like there's anyone to press charges, right?" He meant the comment in jest, but he could tell it confused the reporter a little since he didn't smile at the comment.

The two walked out of the house and over to the barn, where Williams' squad car was parked beside Jenkins' cycle. He had run the motorcycle's plates before he went in the house and had left the radio on, so now it screeched with static.

Jenkins thanked the officer for his understanding and told him to look for the article in Wednesday's edition. Just then his cell phone rang, but he again ignored it. He jumped on his bike and headed for town, filled with dread at the thought of facing Berg when he returned to the office.

He would have sped the entire way were it not for Williams, who followed closely behind him nearly all the way back to the *Messenger* office. It was almost as if he were waiting for Jenkins to exceed the speed limit or fail to signal a turn so he could pop on his cherries and siren and be back in action once again.

12

It was two-forty in the afternoon when Jenkins arrived back at the office. As soon as he stepped through the door, Rachel looked up from a message she was recording from a recent call and they made eye contact. He could tell from her expression that he was in big trouble.

Berg rushed around the corner, his jaws clenched in rage, making the sides of his red face ripple like windswept water.

"Into my office, now!" Berg yelled. He then turned on his heels and stomped off toward his office. Jenkins followed closely behind. He could feel the weight of the stares from Margaret and Frank upon him as he passed by but chose not to look at them. He knew they'd be smiling wryly at him as if to rub in the fact that they were enjoying being witness to a moment they believed was long overdue. He knew they were certain this would be his last day at the *Messenger.*

Once Jenkins was inside the office, Berg slammed the door so hard that it knocked a plaque off the wall, one that recognized the paper's overall achievement of excellence, awarded by the Minnesota Newspaper Association three years earlier. The framed memento tumbled to the ground with the glass splintering into several jagged pieces and scattering about the carpet.

The incident infuriated Berg even further. "Sit down," he ordered, his eyes tethered to Jenkins. "Where have you been?"

But before Jenkins could answer, Berg began his verbal assault that lasted nearly twenty minutes. He brought up every little thing that Jenkins had done over the past several weeks that irritated him, things he had kept bottled up inside...until now. His anger spewed like a raging river. He spent several minutes berating Jenkins for his constant tardiness, the lack of respect he showed everyone in the office, criticized his writing for its lack of emotion, and hammered on his inability to follow certain style guidelines that all newspaper reporters must adhere to.

When his pot had finally boiled over, Berg took a deep breath and sat quietly. He massaged his temples to try to regain his composure.

Then, suddenly, he remembered he was on deadline and that he had to get more pages prepared for layout and final proofing. The thought stressed him even further. He felt a tightening sensation in his chest as he calculated that he was about two hours behind schedule. And Berg hated being behind schedule.

"Where are your stories? I have some large holes to fill, and I don't have your stories. I thought you told me you had them done?"

Jenkins, for once, looked wide-eyed. "I do; they're all done. Well, except the Gutzman piece, but I'm almost finished with that."

"Well, where are they? I looked in the edit folder, and they aren't there."

At the *Messenger*, all computers were networked together so Berg could quickly access everything from his workstation. All editorial and advertising files were saved in a folder on the production computer. There was a folder entitled *Current Issue*, and inside that were seven additional folders: *Steve's Edit*, *John's Edit*, *Calendar Items*, *News Briefs*, *Photos*, *Display Ads*, *Classified Ads*. Every week, Jenkins saved all of his stories in his folder, and Berg opened the file and edited them from his office computer. This week, however, all that was in Jenkins' folder was his crime report and three smaller news items. It was missing the parade story, his coverage of the recent city council meeting, and the Gutzman obituary.

"Oh, man!" Jenkins said, hitting his forehead forcefully with the palm of his hand. "I'm sorry. I worked on them on my laptop and saved them on a disk. It's on my desk. I forgot to transfer them over this morning."

The notion that he could have edited two of the remaining three stories exasperated Berg, and he launched into another tirade during which he scolded Jenkins for his inability to understand his role in the production process.

"There's more to this than you just writing stories," he reminded him sharply. "We have deadlines for a reason, and you know they must be met. I have to edit your work, Margaret has to place it in the paper, and we need to proof it. It all takes time, you know that. And if we don't get it to press on time, that screws up their end as well. When we miss our deadlines there's too much room for error, and that's not acceptable. It's simply not acceptable and I won't stand for it anymore."

Finally, he took one more deep breath and let his tension subside. "Listen, John, I'm afraid this is the last straw. I have no choice but to let you go."

Berg's words hung heavy in the air. It took awhile for Jenkins to grasp what had just been said. He sat in silence for a moment, utterly deflated. Then he summoned his courage and began his defense.

"Steve, listen, I'm really sorry. I know I haven't been the best employee, but I promise I will work at being better. I've never missed a deadline before, have I?"

Berg shook his head.

"It's this Gutzman story," Jenkins tried to explain. "The

thing has consumed me. It seems like everywhere I go I run into someone who has something to say about this guy. I wrote the obituary on Friday, but that was all it was, a simple obituary. I can show it to you and you can run it if you wish, but I've got a lot more information to write a story about who he really was, and I think it's going to be really good. He has an amazing background and had an incredible life. I've been working on it, but I just need a little more time. Can we hold the space?"

Berg was taken aback by Jenkins' remarks. He'd never heard the reporter speak so passionately about an assignment, and he was especially baffled because of the nature of this one: an obituary. Although he didn't want to minimize the severity of the moment, he played along.

"How much time do you need?" he said, glancing at the clock on his wall, which now read 3:17.

"A couple of hours should do it."

Berg sighed deeply and buried his face into his hand as he contemplated whether or not to give Jenkins one more chance.

"Okay, I have a meeting tonight, so I have to leave at five. The story had better be in your edit folder by seven o'clock tomorrow morning," he said sternly, knowing that if he came in early he could edit and place the final story and have the paper proofed and ready for the printer by eleven. "John, this better be worth it."

"It will be. Thanks, Steve," Jenkins said excitedly, a smile stretching from ear to ear. He jumped up and rushed back to his computer to get to work.

As he exited the office, Berg yelled, "And transfer those other files onto our system now!"

All eyes in the office turned toward the remark, and then to John.

The office was filled with commotion as Jenkins pulled out the notes he'd scribbled on the paper tablecloth and those he had taken while reading Gutzman's diaries. The *Messenger* had three phone lines, and every few minutes one of them would light up. Oftentimes, on deadline days, Rachel juggled three incoming calls at once with calm precision. "Good afternoon, the *Messenger*, please hold," she said and pressed the red hold button on her phone. She repeated the simple act until she got to the third caller, whom she transferred and then worked her way back to the other two, always answering the first caller next.

Most of the calls were usually for Frank because many of his clients waited until the last minute to phone in a correction to their ad. It was his responsibility to take the call, get the copy change, and turn it in to Margaret. This was never a happy exchange because Margaret was typically overworked designing pages and making corrections to the editorial copy. When he came to her with a change request, she lowered her eyebrows, whisked the paper from his hand, and read the correction. Most of the time she simply nodded, to let him know she would get to it as soon as possible. There were times when she couldn't read his writing or when a client had made so many revisions that they needed to exchange words. When this happened, Frank smiled mischievously, placed the blame on his client, and left saying, "Remember, Margaret, these ads are our paychecks." The comment always annoyed her...but he was right.

Jenkins tuned out the clatter and got to work. He reread his story from top to bottom, making minor corrections along the way. When he'd come to an area that needed attention and more supporting information, he'd shuffle through the scraps of paper until he found what he was looking for and then insert it into the story.

Before he knew it, Berg was hovering over his shoulder, eyes on the screen. "I'm leaving," he said. "Remember, 7 a.m."

"It'll be done. I promise."

Soon Frank and Rachel were gone, followed closely behind by Margaret. The office fell silent, a welcome relief to Jenkins. He continued writing and revising until the sun set, and the evening darkness enveloped the office. He closed the shade near his desk and kept typing until he massaged the article to his satisfaction.

⌘ ⌘ ⌘

True to his word, Berg arrived sharply at seven o'clock the next morning. The summer sun was already working its way up in the sky, so he turned down the shade on his east-facing window and followed his daily ritual: walk to the coffeepot, pour in the dark grounds, and fill the cistern with water. Grabbing the faxes from the machine, he browsed through them on the way to his office, throwing them in his recycling bin once there or filing the ones he wanted to keep. Next, he checked his voicemail, scribbled down two messages, and turned on his computer to check his emails, which, like the faxes, were mostly unwanted. He responded to the ones that needed immediate attention, then headed back to the coffeepot, which was now about one-third full. Lifting the pot, he poured the thick mixture into his coffee-stained ceramic mug. He loved the dark, bitter flavor of the java that first hit the pot, undiluted by the full measure of water. He returned to his office, opened his word processing program, and mumbled, "It better be here, and it better be good."

Berg clicked through file folders until he came to the one entitled *John's Edit.* He saw the file that simply read *Gutzman Obit,* opened it, and began to read, rapidly breezing through the article to get the flavor of its content. It was his habit to always edit articles by reading them quickly for content once and then going over them a second time much slower, correcting spelling, grammar, and style errors along the way. When he reached the end of his first run-through, he slumped back in his chair, amazed by what he had just read.

How did he get this? he questioned himself. He checked the word count, which set his mind in motion.

At the same time, the rest of the staff was beginning to straggle in. Tuesday morning was the only day of the week that they all arrived before eight. Other than Monday, it was often the busiest and most stressful day of the week as the staff worked feverishly to meet the eleven o'clock deadline. Rachel arrived first, promptly at seven-thirty, followed closely behind by Margaret and Frank. Jenkins was the last to make it through the door, but he was only five minutes behind the others.

When Berg saw Jenkins, he summoned him into his office.

"John, sit down. We need to talk about this article," he said, solemn-faced.

"Don't you like it?" Jenkins asked with a note of disappointment.

"Like it? I love it! I'm shocked, to tell you the truth," Berg said, his hardened demeanor toward Jenkins melting away. "I don't know how you pulled it off, but this is good. Very good."

Jenkins' lips quivered and then finally burst into an ear-to-ear grin, his ego soaking up the compliment like a soothing balm. "I told you it would be worth the wait," he boasted.

"Don't get too cocky yet, John. Now we have a problem. A big problem."

"What's that?"

"Well, because of you and this story I've got to rip apart

some pages. And we need a photo," said Berg, the wheels of his mind now spinning at full speed. The adrenaline, mixed in with his early morning caffeine, was kicking in, giving him an exhilarated feeling that made him feel fully alive. He hated to tear apart pages this late at deadline, but he knew the Gutzman story deserved to be prominently displayed on page one, above the fold. "You were at the funeral. Think hard. Were there any photos displayed there? Anything on the bulletin?"

Jenkins' eyes rolled toward the ceiling as he tried to recall anything that might have contained a photo.

"No. No, Steve. There weren't."

"Oh great! Where can we get a photo? We need a photo. Maybe the church has one in their files. Go call them and—"

"Wait a minute," Jenkins interrupted. "I know where I can get a picture of him and his family. Give me fifteen or twenty minutes, and you'll have your picture. But Steve," he added while standing and getting ready to run out the door, "promise me that if you get a call from the police department, you'll post bail."

"What are you talking about?"

"Never mind. I'll explain it later. I'll be back as soon as possible. I promise."

Berg glanced at his watch, knowing he didn't have time to play a guessing game, so he let him go. He hustled out to the production area.

"Margaret, I hate to tell you this, but we've got a few pages to rework."

"What?" Margaret shot back, fearful she wasn't going to get her work done even without this interruption.

"Sorry," Berg said sympathetically, "but we have to move the council story on page one."

"Page one?" she snapped back, looking at the clock on the

wall and knowing that a redesign of page one meant work on at least one or two other pages as well because of the jumps. She had worked for the *Messenger* for over a dozen years and had never redesigned the front page, much less only two hours before sending the paper to the printer.

"Yes, page one," said Berg. "I need about a 1,700 word hole. Any suggestions on where we can jump it?"

Margaret's eyes opened wide. Most of the articles in the *Messenger* were between 500 and 750 words, so she knew she'd have to rework at least three pages to make it fit. She sighed deeply and began clicking through the layout pages on her screen while Berg peered over her shoulder. "The council story jumps to two, but that's only, what, about 500 words?"

Berg studied the page, then told her to zoom out so he could see page three as well. Page three always held the community calendar, which listed the weekly events of the local clubs and organizations, everything from churches to the library to social service clubs. He told her to click through the other pages of the paper slowly. As she did, he searched for the easiest place to pull an article so the current page one jump could be moved. However, the puzzle was fit tightly together, and there wasn't an easy option.

"Go back to page three," he said matter-of-factly.

Margaret looked at him in disbelief, then bent her neck to look directly at him as if to say, "Page three? Are you crazy?"

"Take out the calendar," he said sternly. "Move the entire council story to three, along with the riverfront development jump. Rework page one so this Gutzman article is on top, with space for a four-column picture." He paused and then changed his mind because he didn't know how good of a picture that Jenkins would bring back. "Wait. Make it a three-column picture. Jump the story to two. Hopefully we'll have room."

Margaret clicked to page three and highlighted the calendar. She looked at Berg one more time for confirmation and, getting another nod, hit *Delete.* Berg sighed, knowing he would hear about that move from nearly every organization in town Wednesday afternoon after the paper was published.

With the gravity of the act still hanging heavy in the air, Frank came scurrying over, ecstatic. "Hey, great news! The pharmacy wants to run a quarter page. It's the same one they ran last week, with just some minor changes. Can we get them in?" he asked, fully expecting to know the answer.

Although he was supposed to have all ads finalized by noon each Monday, it was common for him to slide in a smaller ad or two at the eleventh hour. However, it was rare that he would reel in such a large ad this late in the game, and one that produced such a substantial amount of revenue.

Berg's spirit sank, knowing what he had to do. "Sorry, Frank. We can't do it," he said, eyeing him only briefly and then Margaret, who was ready to pounce on him like an angry lioness if he agreed.

"Steve, a quarter page! Isn't there something we can do?" Frank pleaded, dumbfounded at his unwillingness to even look for space as he normally did. "I already told him I was sure we could do it."

"Sorry, but we're already reworking three pages. We don't have time or space. We're tight. Really tight. Tell Charlie we're sorry and that we'll get it in next week."

Berg walked slowly back to his office, trying not to think about how that ad would have covered this month's phone and light bills.

Moments later, Jenkins arrived with a framed portrait under his arm. Margaret scanned it, placed it on page one, and printed out the first three pages for a final proof. Berg looked them over, doublechecked the headlines, then told Margaret to create the final electronic file and email it to the printer. It was 11:03.

13

For the past ten minutes, Chuck Benson had been frequently checking his computer to see if the *Messenger* had sent its pages. It was after eleven o'clock, and he normally had the paper's file by now. He was beginning to get anxious. Working in the pre-press department of the printing plant, it was Benson's job to review the file before sending it to the pressroom. The *Messenger* was the first of three newspapers that he would preview today, each taking about an hour, and he was fearful that he would get behind schedule if it didn't arrive soon.

He picked up the phone to call Berg. Cradling the receiver between his shoulder and cheek, Chuck punched the telephone keypad while keeping one eye on his computer. Before he hit the last number, the file suddenly appeared.

Hanging up the phone quickly, Chuck got to work. He grabbed the production order hanging on a nearby clipboard and scanned the file to make sure the page counts matched. Next, he checked the color pages, of which there were only two. Page one had full-color process, and the back page contained a full-page grocery store ad that used only one color: red.

Finally, he went through the file, page by page, and placed it into his prepress program. When finished, he sent it to the pressroom and then checked his computer for the file of his next paper, which wasn't yet there.

The paper was printed at a central plant about one hour away from Marquette. It had been done that way since the late 1980s, when the *Messenger* surrendered its antiquated press to the scrap yard after the publisher determined it was cheaper to contract out the work than to buy a new and very expensive printing press. The company that printed the paper owned three weekly newspapers of its own and had established a niche of printing papers for several other smaller publishers. All of its clients were far enough away as to not compete for each other's advertising revenue, so it was a situation that worked well for all parties.

The press made a monotonous droning as it whisked the long, thin sheet of newsprint from its massive spindle and then snaked it through several wide ebony rollers that inked its content on the newsprint. What began as a blank sheet of paper at one end of the large, blocky press was transformed into the *Messenger* on the other end. Once the finished product was off the press, it was cut and folded and ended up on a conveyor belt in the same form that it would look like when it arrived on the doorstep of every subscriber in Marquette.

A long-haired thirty-year-old with ink-stained hands watched as the first few issues rolled off. He picked up a copy, examined the color and registration, and barked an order to another pressman to make an adjustment. A few seconds later he grabbed another paper, looked it over, and gave a thumbs-up sign to his coworker.

With that, the press was fired up to do its work, rolling out the full number of copies in a matter of minutes. Once off the press, the papers were machine-tied in bundles of fifty and loaded onto a delivery truck for Marquette.

⌘ ⌘ ⌘

At four-thirty that afternoon, a large white truck with a faded printing company logo on its side drove down an alley and pulled up to the loading dock of the *Messenger* office, precisely on schedule. Berg was there to watch the driver maneuver the truck down the long, narrow passageway and into place. The driver hopped out, exchanged small talk with Berg, and then began unloading the newspapers. He used a hand-jack to hoist a pallet off the truck bed and then rolled it down a long metal ramp, making a shrilling sound along the way. He steered it into the back of the *Messenger* office, dropped it down on the ground, and left it there for Berg to deal with. The pallet of papers was shrink-wrapped and contained 50 bundles that were layered on top of each other like a fine masonry wall.

As the driver got into his truck, Berg was already tearing away the shrink-wrap.

With the smell of diesel still lingering in the air from the delivery truck, the first of the newspaper carriers' parents began to arrive. Soon there was a line of minivans, SUVs, and pickups stretching down the entire length of the alley. Each driver waited patiently as the one ahead pulled up to the dock, grabbed three or four bundles, and threw them into his or her vehicle and sped away. The line was fast and efficient, with no one taking more than one minute to complete the task.

By 5:15 p.m., all of the papers were out of the office and ready for distribution. Berg often commented at community events that he had the hardest working youth of Marquette working for him, when in reality he knew that many of the routes were assisted by the kids' parents, and others were even completely done by them because their kids were either too tired or busy or lazy to get the job done by 8:00 p.m., as required.

⌘⌘⌘

Ben Schultz, a skinny redheaded, freckle-faced entrepreneurial twelve-year-old, took his paper route very seriously. He had been delivering the six-square block neighborhood between Fourth and Tenth streets for over two years, taking it over from his older brother, Jim. Having learned the route from his elder sibling and making a few efficiency adjustments of his own, he now had it down to a science and could complete the route in less than two hours nearly every week, weather permitting. He earned eighty dollars for his efforts, most of which he was saving for large purchases, like his most recent investment of an iPod. It was a quarter after six when he dropped the *Messenger* on the doorstep of Elmer and Sally Crosser's home.

Elmer, a bent man in his late eighties, was peering through a linen curtain to make sure the paperboy put the paper exactly where he told him it should go: top step, to the right of the door so he wouldn't push it away when he opened the screen door.

Ben landed the paper perfectly in its requested position from ten feet away while in full stride, just like he did every week. Elmer shook his head; he'd secretly hoped the boy would miss so he could call and complain and give himself justification for never tipping Ben, even at Christmastime, when Berg ran a full-page promotional ad encouraging the gesture. Elmer shuffled to the door, opened it slowly, and retrieved his paper.

"Is that the paper?" called Sally from the kitchen in a high, mousy voice.

She was scraping burnt ketchup and hamburger from a pan she'd used to cook a meatloaf dinner. Although she had a dishwasher, she usually hand-washed and dried her dishes after each meal and put them away in the cupboard since she has little else to do in the evenings.

"Of course it is. What else would I be doing at the door?" Elmer snapped back.

Sally didn't respond to his snide remark.

With the paper under his arm, Elmer limped back to his recliner, turned around slowly, and eased himself into the chair. He clutched the lever and extended the footrest, giving relief to his aching legs. His cane, which he needed to walk long distances, was resting by the chair.

"Humph," he muttered as he pulled the paper to him and unfolded it. "Oh, for crying out loud," he grumbled loudly when he saw the front page.

"What's wrong?" asked Sally, scurrying to the living room from the kitchen as fast as her 87-year-old legs could carry her.

"Would you look at this?" he said, slapping the paper with the back of his hand. "They did a story on Gutzman, and they put it on the front page!"

"Oh dear. I thought it was something serious."

"Serious? I doubt there is *anything* serious happening in town if this is the only thing they have to put on the front page."

Elmer rested the paper in his lap and pulled a lighter and a pack of cigarettes from his blue denim shirt pocket. He tapped the bottom of the pack sharply three times on the wrinkled palm of his hand and then shook it lightly until a long, white cigarette protruded from the package. With gnarled fingertips stiff with arthritis, he plucked the cigarette out and put it between his lips, letting it dangle downward. His stubby thumb sparked his lighter, producing a tall, orange flame, which he put to the cigarette. He drew in a long, deep breath, held it for a moment, and then exhaled the warm, pungent smoke.

Although Sally was an impeccable housekeeper, the entire house reeked of stale smoke from Elmer's chain-smoking habit.

She hated his habit and the effect it had on his health and on their home.

Watching the scene, and her husband's disgust, she retreated to the kitchen, knowing he wanted to be alone with his paper. She'd learned a long time ago that arguing wasn't worth it.

Pouring herself a cup of coffee, she sat down at the table and began her early evening ritual: she dealt out a game of solitaire.

Elmer picked up his paper, unfolded it, and sneered again at the headline about Alfred Gutzman. It put him in a foul mood, which wasn't hard to do. Elmer had spent his entire adult life angry at the world, but he hadn't always been that way.

When he and Sally met, he had been young and ambitious and full of dreams, which he shared with her often. They fell in love instantly and were married at an early age, just weeks before the beginning of WWII. Ever the patriot, he was one of the first men from Marquette to enlist in the Army when the war broke out. It was an experience that would change his life forever.

As a soldier, Elmer saw and participated in more killing and brutal acts of war than he could handle. One day, following a particularly fierce battle, he had a nervous breakdown due to battle fatigue. He was found weeping uncontrollably, clinging to a tree so tightly that it took three men to pry him away from it. He was taken from the front line to an Army hospital, where he was evaluated and found unfit for further military service.

The war ended before his hospital stay was over, so he was discharged honorably due to his service accomplishments, for which he was highly decorated. However, there were other boys from Marquette in his unit, and they shared word of his breakdown with their families back home. Because the news preceded his arrival, he had returned home in shame.

Sally had tried for years to soften the sting of Elmer's shame after the war, but the experience had created a hard callous on his heart. No one—not even her—could get through.

Having been deeply in love with him before the war, it devastated her to see what the war had done to him. She had vowed, all those years ago, to remain by his side, even though that meant she was most often the target of his aggression. There were many nights when she'd wept bitterly, watching him thrash about from horrible nightmares, battling his demons within.

Despite the way he treated her, she still loved him. She knew he loved her, too…but had long forgotten how to show it.

"Humph," Elmer growled as he began to read the article.

About three paragraphs into the story, he shouted loud enough for Sally to hear, "I knew it!"

"What's that, dear?" she replied softly.

"He was a Kraut. Gutzman *was* a Kraut!"

"Oh dear," she said. She wished he wouldn't read anymore of the article because she feared it might trigger painful memories.

"I knew it," he said again. "I never did trust him."

With that statement he became lost in the memory of the first time he met Gutzman. It was shortly after the end of the war and both were playing on a church softball league; Gutzman for St. Paul's, and Elmer for St. Mary's, the Catholic church in town. The two teams had developed a friendly rivalry, facing each other in the league championship for the past six of seven years. The Lutherans were up four games to

144

three, including a win the previous year, so they were defending their bragging rights. Gutzman was playing catcher that day when Elmer stepped up to the plate. It was the top of the ninth with the score tied 4-4, and two outs. The Catholics were confident they would get a victory because Elmer was their best hitter....

⌘⌘⌘

"One more, Tommy. You can do this," Gutzman called out toward the pitching mound as he crouched down into position, putting his thick padded glove in front of him and his right arm behind his back.

Elmer could detect the man's German accent immediately and the sound of it instantly made his blood boil. He planted his feet shoulder-width apart, cocked the bat, and swung wildly at the first pitch.

"Strike one!" shouted the umpire, a neutral Methodist.

"Way to go, Tommy," said Gutzman as he pulled the ball from his glove and hurled it back to the mound. "Two more. We need two more just like that."

Elmer sneered at him and dug his feet deeper into the dirt. He took a powerful practice swing, showing great form, with his torso twisting easily and his bat making a full rotation around his back.

The pitcher lobbed his second pitch toward home plate and again Elmer swung hard.

"Strike two!"

The Lutherans cheered while the Catholics looked on with growing concern.

"That's the way, Tommy. Just one more," said Gutzman as he threw the ball back to him.

Every time Elmer heard Gutzman's accent, his anger

bubbled closer to the surface. He dug in, cocked the bat, and stepped into the next pitch as he watched the white ball float in and make contact with the end of his bat. He hit it squarely, and it sailed deep into left field, over the head of the outfielder. It hit the top of the fence, missing being a homerun by inches.

With strong, powerful legs, Elmer sprinted toward first base, barely touching the bag so as not to lose momentum, and then ran on to second. As he rounded that base, he saw the outfielder bobble the ball so he knew he could make a play for home. As he rounded third, the fielder threw the ball to the shortstop, who caught it, turned around quickly, and fired it to home plate. Seeing he might not beat the throw, Elmer lowered his shoulder and barreled into Gutzman as he caught the ball, knocking him to the ground. The Lutherans jumped up from their bench and screamed at the overly aggressive play as the Catholics stood silently, stunned by what they had just seen.

Gutzman was lying on the ground, curled up in the fetal position to ease the pain in his stomach and shoulder. Elmer stood tall over him, staring arrogantly down at him. The umpire rushed in and pulled him away. Gutzman got to his knees, and then to his feet, as his teammates crowded around him to see if he was injured. Blood was trickling down to his hand from a large scrape on his forearm. He opened his glove, took out the ball with his bloodstained hand, and turned toward Elmer.

"You're out," he said softly yet firmly, looking him directly in the eyes. He dropped the ball and walked away....

⌘⌘⌘

Elmer shook the memory from his mind and continued reading the article. The light was beginning to dim in the house, so he pulled the paper closer to him so he could better see and digest all that it said. When he read about Gutzman's personal tragedy during the tornado and of how it damaged his farm, he muttered under his breath, "I remember that day. There were a lot of other farms that were hit worse than his." Jenkins' tribute to Gutzman for his acts of compassion that he showed to people like Sandy, the waitress from the Corner Cupboard, also made him scoff.

However, when he came to the portion about Gutzman's military experience, he read with great interest about his time at the concentration camp and of his desertion. He finished the article and then returned to that portion and reread it, not once, but twice. He dropped the paper in his lap and stared blankly into space, small tears forming in eyes that had been dry for over fifty years.

Sally, who was still sitting at the kitchen table playing solitaire, was suddenly aware her husband's grumbling had stopped, and there was an eerie silence in the home. Alarmed, she rushed to the doorway that separated the kitchen from the living room. Elmer was sitting in his chair. She could instantly see that his eyes were moist and red.

"Are you okay?" she asked. "Oh heavens, what's wrong? Is everything all right?"

Elmer put the paper on the end table and wiped the tears from his eyes with the knuckles of both pointer fingers. He returned the footrest of his recliner to the closed position and stood up slowly, bracing himself with both hands on the arms of the chair.

"Humph," he muttered as he grabbed his cane and again wiped his teary eyes. He gently put his hand on Sally's shoulder as he hobbled past her on the way to his bedroom, realizing for the first time just how deep his war wounds really were.

Epilogue

Orange, crimson, and gold maple leaves were swirling around the parking lot when the first of the fans arrived for the home opener of the Marquette Mavericks. Soon a long line of people gathered at the ticket booth, waiting to pay nine dollars each to see their football team take on its conference rival.

At quarter to seven, the home bleachers were completely filled with fans, many of them dressed in green and white. The visitor's side was over two-thirds filled, which was remarkable considering the distance those fans had to travel. They were sporting their school colors as well. Both sides were teeming with energy and anticipation as they awaited the kick-off. The temperature was dropping quickly as the sun sank into the horizon, and those in heavy jackets pulled up their zippers and put on their stocking caps and mittens or gloves. The high school youth were dressed in hooded sweatshirts and jeans and huddled around each other, undeterred by the nip in the air. They talked and laughed and whispered and gossiped, concerned more with their social life than the game about to take place.

In the crowd was John and Rachel Jenkins. John was looking around nervously for Pete Hancock, a retired athletic director from Marquette High School who now freelanced for him covering sporting events for the *Messenger*. Jenkins spied him on the sideline, fiddling with the long lens of his camera, and breathed a sigh of relief. He knew that if Hancock didn't arrive, he'd have to rush back to his car and get his camera and

148

cover the game himself.

The PA announcer asked the crowd to rise and join the senior jazz quartet in singing the national anthem. Before the last note, the crowd hooted and whistled and made muffled clapping sounds with their mitted hands. When the crowd noise subsided, the announcer turned on his microphone, with a familiar pop and screech.

"Welcome to Gutzman Field, home of the Marquette Mavericks," he said exuberantly, filling the crowd with adrenaline. "Tonight the Mavericks play host to the Goodhue Wildcats, a conference game. Now, please stand and welcome your Mavericks."

With that, the pep band let loose with their horns and drums, and the hulky, muscular football players darted out from between the bleachers and took the field, bursting through a large green and white banner with the school's mascot on it that was being held by two long-legged cheerleaders who smiled broadly. The players circled around each other and jumped up and down, hitting each other on their helmets and shoulder pads, while grunting unintelligible words. The coaches took their usual position at the fifty-yard line and continued discussing their opening strategy.

Sitting next to Jenkins was Patrick Norberg, head of the football boosters. He was educating Jenkins on the starting lineup, quoting the height, weight, and tackles or yardage gained by each starting player during the previous season. As the players lined up on the lush, green turf opposite each other for the kick-off, Norberg leaned close to Jenkins. "There's something about Coach Hallberg that I think you should know about. I think it'd make for a great read in your paper."

"What's that?" replied Jenkins, certain Norberg merely wanted a feature story on the football team that would shine a bright light on the booster club.

Norberg leaned close to Jenkins and talked soft and low so

those around him couldn't hear what he was saying, including Rachel, who was bending her ear to the conversation while pretending to be interested in what Norberg's wife was saying to her.

Jenkins snapped his head back, and his eyes grew wide as he processed the information he'd just learned. He sat up straight, turned his body toward Norberg, and then looked him directly in the eye.

"Really! That *is* interesting."

About the Author

TIM SPITZACK is editor and publisher of a newspaper publishing company in St. Paul, Minnesota. He has a B.S. degree in Journalism and Sociology and over twenty years' experience working in community journalism.

"There's a popular phrase in community journalism that says there are no bad stories, only bad writers. What this means is that there are a multitude of interesting stories about our fellow citizens to discover if we are willing to scratch below the surface. I wrote *The Messenger* to pay tribute to the people who live quiet lives, but through their acts of love and compassion influence the lives of so many others."

www.timspitzack.com
www.oaktara.com

LaVergne, TN USA
07 December 2010
207781LV00005B/138/P